The Fool's Bouquet

I just want to thank Sarah.
I wrote this for you.
You are an utterly amazing person.

Jackson Farway

The Fool's Bouquet

Bibliographic information published by the Deutsche Nationalbibliothek
The Deutsche Nationalbibliothek lists this publication in the Deutsche Nationalbibliografie; detailed bibliographic data are available in the Internet at https://dnb.dnb.de.

Verlag: BoD • Books on Demand GmbH,
In de Tarpen 42, 22848 Norderstedt
Druck: Libri Plureos GmbH, Friedensallee 273, 22763 Hamburg

ISBN: 978-3-7597-2428-1

The Fool's Bouquet

This will be an account from my life, inspired by another book. A book that I have not even finished reading yet. One that I have dreaded reading for a long time, because a better man would hate the experience. Alas, I find myself very entertained so far and I am enjoying even some scenes that are meant to be off-putting and certainly were not intended to invoke any nostalgia in the reader.

We are speaking of Vladimir Nabakov's acclaimed "Lolita".

The astute reader will find similarities to that timeless story in this account.

The similarities in the language are - with purpose - an imitation. The book was lent to me by a good friend who was appropriately horrified by the content. Quite possibly more horrified than the creator had intended, for her disgust made her give the book away after reading less than a third of it. I fought another friend over the right to receive the little tome and won (this is a very embellished retelling).

In any case, the original owner later asked me about my opinion on the book. At the time, I had been rather annoyed with the language employed. She fervently disagreed with me there, explaining how the language had been the most enjoyable, possibly the only enjoyable part of her short journey with Humbert Humbert.

I have come around to see her point. In my defense, the beginning of the book has nothing of importance happening. The reader has exposition thrown at him that may or may not gain some value with further exploration of the tale told. When reading those parts, you develop a nagging feeling that you are reading words barely worth reading or remembering.

This was done in an exceedingly verbose manner. The simple truth is: The early part uses many words to say very little of relevance. Now that I have reached the parts where it uses those many words to describe exactly the story you expected to be reading, I also find myself enamored with the prose.

Hence the similarities in language. One may accuse me of trying to impress said friend, and I must vehemently deny that, if only because she will be among the first to ever read this.

There will also be similarities in some of the scenes described. That is much easier to explain. What you are about to read is a true story. A tale full of memories that keep me awake at night, regretting things done and wishing death upon myself for things not done. This will be a book without a satisfying ending - as is to be expected of true stories and most certainly of one taken from my life. And some events of my life just happen to mirror events from that other book.

Before we begin, allow me to paint you the full

picture of the narrator. Imagine a man just past thirty, sitting in a sparsely adorned room, two monitors in a corner the only sources of light during this rainy night. The man is full of frustrations. For one, he was recently abandoned by a romantic interest. Dumped with an excuse that sounded sensible, but was disproved as an untruth a mere week later. He has always been a trusting fellow.

Another noteworthy and recent loss would be that of his employment. He might defiantly think "good riddance" to that, but particularly the older members of his family voiced fears of the negative effect that "having too much time" has on the mental health of a person. For now, this author and narrator is very much enjoying his free time, but there is a small voice in the back of his head that shares the concerns of the concerned.

What seems grim already is reinforced by a recently acquired injury. An impact onto the ribcage slightly repositioned one of the ribs. The pain is manageable, but not constant and it keeps surprising the poor fellow. It is bad enough to be depressing, but not actually so bad as to be worth complaining or even worrying about.

Sleep has, as one would assume, suffered greatly under the psychological and physical pains.

The waking hours are spent on an online

game. He has set a target rank and the dedicated labour to reach it has proved to be sufficient distraction to forget his mental woes while staying unmoving enough to ignore the impacted ribcage. Said targeted rank was reached only hours before these words were written. The triumph was very shortlived. Sometimes you reach a goal and it only leaves you empty and bereft of goals.

I should not complain. Reaching a goal and finding it empty is an experience that is, while disheartening, far less displeasing than the feelings you explore when not reaching your goals at all. Coincidentally, that will be an important theme of the story you are about to read.

Best get on with it then.

So where do we start? At the beginning, I suppose.

The day in question is rather easy to pinpoint. I do not have the date at hand, although that could be researched. But, to the consternation of many friends and family members, I am a slouch and thus unwilling to do said research. Suffice to say, it was late November or early December in 2019. Back when the world was blissfully unaware of the dangers posed by the smallest of nonliving organisms, back when Chinese people could eat as many flying rodents as they wanted and no one would bat an eye. Except, maybe, probably, animal rights activists. But yes, the horrors of global pandemic remained yet a few months into the future. Much more immediately lurking in the shallows of our calendars was the yearly recurring birth of Christ. As is tradition, you meet the important and cherished people in your life at Christmas eve and the following days. Remaining acquaintances are slotted into the weeks prior. One such slot was the Christmas party in our local dancing school

I attended together with my loving, caring, sweet and beautiful girlfriend of the time.

I had first met her in the same building, at a dancing event. We both weekly attended several dancing lessons and trainings, as well as social dance evenings. The school was somewhat of a second home to us and we loved many of the people there like family. It was a place of comfort and warmth for both of us.

I loved her. And in many ways, I still do.

For this story to make sense, it is imperial that I describe my girlfriend's position and relevance in my life. This relationship was fertile soil for all the feelings developed and all the connections formed over the course of this story. It was the biggest hurdle to overcome in the struggle caused by that fateful evening and it would be the greatest solace in the aftermath.

I can confidently say that the time I spent with my girlfriend, which lasted a bit more than seven years, was the happiest period of my life. A superstitious part of me likens it to the old testament, where seven years of fertility and surplus are followed by seven years of draught and scarcity. I am by no means a religious person, but there is, in that comparison, a hope that I want to cling to. The hope that my current state of mind will only last for five more years.

I still vividly remember the moment I first met her. Rose (that was not her name, obviously. But for anonymity's sake, I will invent pseudonyms for everyone appearing in this story) was standing on the dancefloor, with a friend of hers that I would come to loathe in the following years. They were positioned perfectly to block the way of those dancing slow waltz around them and themselves blissfully unaware of the inconvenience they were causing. I approached them and asked Rose whether she wanted to dance with me. She declined, saying she was talking to her friend and would not interrupt the conversation right now. Ever polite and considerate of the limits imposed by a girl, I took that rejection as you should take any rejection and did not approach her again.

Instead, she did the approaching, hours later when everyone was changing back into winterproof outdoor-shoes after the end of the event.

"Oh no, now we've missed each other for the rest of the evening! I would really have liked to dance with you."

What followed were sweet texts sent to one another, with innocent flirting and promises of dancing at the next event. These promises were kept and a date followed soon thereafter. That date had to remain kissless, as she was still in a relationship, but it quickly became a physically intimate evening even without our lips touching. I can still see the moment I relinquished her to the streetcar, saying "you will regret this (not kissing) the moment these doors close. You will spend the whole weekend imagining how it would have felt." And, with a sheepish grin on my face, I added that she will deserve that anguish.

My prediction proved true and first thing on Monday she broke up with her poor fellow and asked me to meet her again in the evening.

What followed was the beginning of a sweet and youthful love. A relationship fueled by admiration, affection, lust, desire, trust… we had amazing chemistry, kept no secrets from one another and we were completely unable to keep our hands off each other's body.

Very soon, between the pillows and the blankets, I laid a groundwork that would define our connection in the years to come.

"I love you. I want to spend my while life with you, want to feel like this for the rest of my days and years. But you are the first woman in my life. And while I can imagine spending my whole life with you, I cannot see myself knowing only one woman until I die."

So I broached the subject of an open relationship. We would both only know one true love, but other people were allowed into our lives and beds. I was romantic about it, saying that feelings are inevitable and suppressing them would bring more grief than allowing one another to act on them. I told her I was terrified that this relationship would one day end because of someone else. I quoted examples from my family, from history, from fiction, all of them retelling a single truth that has plagued humanity for millenia: Loving a person does not prevent one from falling in love with someone else. In a less romantic moment, I also told her that one man could not possibly satisfy her carnal desires on his own, me panting in the sheets and unable to move, her already up and ready to go again.

To this day, I do not know if she agreed to it because she was scared to lose me if she refused or whether she saw the truth of what I said and embraced it because she wanted to. At the time, I was convinced of the latter. Nowadays, I'm rather certain it was a mixture of both.

She was fifteen years old when I met her and I was twenty-two.

In the following years, she would live the dream of polygamy, extensively. I will spare you the details, but when crusty old ladies sit in a café, watching young women pass by and they say "if I looked like that again, I would do…" rest assured that Rose has done it. She lived that life that most women don't even dare imagine and she had my full support and encouragement. I wanted her to be happy, I wanted her to be satisfied and I derived a great satisfaction from the fact that she would always return to me after trying someone else and finding them lacking in comparison.

Myself, I… got less mileage out of the arrangement. A kiss, here and there. Some indecent touching. Enough to break up a normal relationship over, but never any penetrative intercourse. Easily explained, of course. Rose got men interested by entering the room. That is all she ever had to do. They wanted her body, they realized they could have it, they enjoyed it and then they were happy about it.

That approach did not work for me. Make no mistake, I also got girls interested in me, but with my mannerisms. With the way I talked. With the way my friends looked at me, the way I lead the girls over the dancefloor, the way I smiled at them, the way I controlled and held a conversation and with the warmth I carried into every friendship. In short, I made them fall in love. And when the time came to make those fantasies of love come true, when my hands traveled to forbidden places and my lips found theirs at last… they said that this would only hurt them. That they could not accept not being my true love. That they wanted to be my number one.

I know I could have had them anyway. Either by ignoring their feeble "this is too much" and "I don't think this is a good idea" and keeping my hands exactly where they were… Or by lying to them, telling them they could eventually, maybe, replace Rose.

But, as established, I was always one to respect a rejection. I kept to the truth and removed my hands.

I did that because I had all I ever needed. Rose loved me with all her heart. She brought warmth and happiness into my life. She made me laugh on a grumpy day, made me smile just by being there, made me enjoy the mornings when I woke up next to her and made me look forward to every second I could spend in her presence. Anyone else would only be a bonus. A coveted and desired bonus, yes, but if they feared that I would only hurt their feelings in the end, then that was not a pain worth risking. I lost nothing.

Such was the state of our relationship when we entered that fateful Christmas celebration.

It is such a warm and glowing memory to me. Everyone is laughing when I picture it. Sitting at the tables, drinking sweet punch and wine, eating little pastries or cake, talking and smiling… Everyone applauded when the results of the year's dancing competitions were read out and prizes distributed accordingly.

One friend, we will call him Diego, was in a bad spot emotionally and needed a break from all the noise and people. He sought that respite in one of the training rooms, hooked his phone into the speakers there and played some of his favorite music. I followed him, knowing that we were good enough friends for him to tolerate my presence in this moment of deliberate solitude and I had tact enough to not say anything as we stood in the darkness, lit only by the streetlights outside, fully immersed in the beats and melodies…

If a genie ever decides to grant me a wish, I will wish to go back to that moment.

Slowly, our close friends trickled into the room. These were the kind of people that would quickly notice our absence and miss us dearly. The ones that knew us well enough to guess correctly where we were, what we were doing and wanted to share the moment. Oh what a roll of heroes we were. A secret little in-group, formed spontaneously by the desire of one man to be alone - and the people he could enjoy being alone with.

But there is nothing more attractive than a secret, and this one was no exception. The door would open and close again and again, slowly transitioning this moment of tranquility into another one of merry enjoyment, of group interaction. It was still a very happy time, make no mistake, but the spell was gone and replaced by something else.

One can argue that my Rose was one of the people who belonged into those first magical and tranquil minutes, although staying silent had never been her strong suit. In any case, she arrived later, when the spell was already broken, or at least in the process of breaking.

She brought a friend with her, into that room. Into my life. And introduced her to me.

I had seen Lily before (you will not gleam her actual name from me either). She had been part of the children dance training organized by our dance school and had performed at tournaments held there.

But some people only exist in the peripherals of your life. You see them. You recognize them. But you do not actually realize they are there. Like people stopping at the same traffic light as you. You somewhat need to engage with them and consider them in your immediate decisions, but you do not register them as people, as humans. They are as inanimate as the red standing man and the green walking one.

Lily had been like that, to me. Some kid that danced, on a floor of dancing kids.

There are people who will badmouth me, saying I like children, am attracted to little girls. Some of the readers will even agree, at the end of this story. But I must vehemently deny it. I have never desired anyone who would not be capable of desiring me back. I would never indecently touch someone who does not understand the meaning and intention behind that touch and is not mature enough to either reciprocate or deny my attempts at affection and attention.

So her dancing in these competitions not only did not interest me, it never even registered in my brain. I knew she existed, but only barely.

Until she stood in front of me, introduced by Rose.

She looked simultaneously shy and eager to meet me. Her eyes said "I have heard so much of you" and they clearly liked what they saw.

Rose said that they were good friends, that she saw her as a bit of a younger sister and that it was time for us to finally know each other. Pleasantries were exchanged. The music at that point had become very dance-able and we were all instinctively arranged in a circle, just moving our bodies along the beat.

And seeing Lily's movement made my head swim. Puberty had hit her in the hips and chest.

In the way she carried herself and in the way she looked at her surroundings. She was aware of me looking at her and her movement responded to that attention, perfectly in sync with the music and with the rhythm of my heart. She had graduated from childhood - at least to my eyes.

Now these circles of people tend to adjust. At first, there were three people between her and me. But the natural forces of attraction led us to come closer to one another, every time someone exited the circle, every time some of the space between us opened up, until it was only Rose standing between us. Who then also left, presumably to get a drink, or a snack, or talk to that guy she had a massive crush on. I do not know where she went.

Have you ever held two magnets close to one another, slowly decreasing the distance between them until you reach that point where the forces grow too strong to suppress and the just CLACK together?

All I know is that I was holding Lily's hands, our eyes were locked and our hips moved in completely symmetrical shapes when Rose returned. Now mind you, the only thing touching was our hands. We were not glued to one another and grinding our bodies against each other. I know I would have wanted to, and I also know now that she felt the same way. But we barely knew one another, we were in a room with other people and there was a considerable age gap between us. So no, we were not touching indecently when Rose came back and saw us there. But we did not need to.

"No! Absolutely not! Not you two! No!"

And I hate to admit that these magical words are what sealed my fate.

The fruit had already been sweet. But now it was also forbidden.

I honestly do not remember how we reacted. I know we did not deny that we found each other interesting. I know we did not ridicule Rose by saying she was overreacting. We just… accepted the way she felt about it, vaguely reassured her that we only wanted to know each other and that this was why she had introduced us, no? After all, neither of us fully understood the gravity of our feelings. Yet.

The rest of the evening gets hazy in my memory. I remember Lily asking me why she doesn't see me at the dancing school more often. I explained to her that dancing was more of a social thing to me than a sport and that I had no dance partner to train with anyway. She said she'd love to see me more often. I asked how she got here and what she would be doing after the evening was over. She said her dance partner and ex-boyfriend, who was also her neighbor, had driven her here and would take her back home. I had felt someone's jealous stare throughout the evening and now knew the why behind it. I remained unbothered. Let the fool be jealous, he had obviously had his chance and squandered it.

Near the end of the evening, I remember Lily and I were cuddling on the stairs, her standing a bit higher than me to mitigate the difference in height. I asked her if it wasn't too warm to wear a hoodie with long sleeves in here, clearly indicating that I would love to undress her. She said that she did in fact feel hot, but wasn't wearing anything underneath.

"And you need the long sleeves to hide the scars, don't you?" She did not reply to that. But now, years later, I know that these were the magical words that sealed *her* fate. That this was the moment she felt understood and felt respected, on top of all the natural chemistry we were already experiencing.

Her nagging ex could not contain his jealousy any longer and convinced her to finally come and go home already. We said our goodbyes with a very long embrace, both saying we'd love to see each other more often… and then she was gone.

Rose took my arm, snuggled against me and after a long kiss told me that I looked very happy.

Through all that will come, I need to stress this: She already felt dread back then, seeing Lily and me on those stairs, sharing each other's warmth and enjoying a moment of bliss and comfort. I know it was unsettling to her, a dark premonition. But she later said that she had nonetheless not wanted to interfere because both of us looked so happy. Because, after all, she had wanted us to get along.

Rose was the love of my life. A kind and beautiful person, inside and out. It is impossible for me to imagine ever again loving someone the way I loved her. The rational part of me knows, of course, that it will happen anyway. Claiming that I will never love anyone the way I loved Rose is like claiming "I will never drink too much again!"

It's funny how our feelings and our knowledge always disagree.

Almost always, at least. For there is one thing that both my rational brain and my emotional heart know without doubt: I will never again fall in love the way I fell in love with Lily.

As a writer, I have to say that this is a novel experience for me. Half my life now, I have been writing fantasy stories as a hobby and I have spent these years facing roadblock after roadblock. Whenever I finally moved past an important part of the story, or finished that scene I'd been working towards for months... I always fell into this hole of not knowing how to continue.

The general story, of course, is mapped in my brain. But it's the actual steps to take, the scenes to show and the dialogue you include that set the head spinning for weeks. I've had month-long phases of not writing anything because I just did not know how to continue at the particular junction.

No such worries trouble me with this account you are reading. Life already wrote the story and I am only recording it for posterity.

I begin to envy all those celebrities who make money with their biographies.

I would love to ridicule them for taking the easy road, but then again I am walking that same road right now.

On the way home from that merry celebration, Rose began to tell me more about Lily. I remember being frustrated at her because she was clearly trying to dissuade me from having further contact with the girl, but she was doing it in such a vague way that the secrecy only served to make it even more enticing to me.

"She's a sweet girl, I know, but such a troubled child."

"I am happy you get along, but I fear she would drag you into her... problems."

"I love how close you've gotten, but try not to get too close. She would burn you and I don't want to see you hurt."

"I just hope she won't bother you with the more disturbing stories from her life. It really is nothing she should be sharing with people."

This made me simultaneously angry at her for trying to drive a wedge inbetween Lily and me, as well as her clumsiness at doing it.

But I was a good boyfriend. I did not seek out Lily on social media, which would have been rather easy. I did not contact her at all.

I filed that evening under "cherished memories" and the girl under "vague acquaintances" and this concluded the story for me.

Lily contacted me the very next day, around noon, and asked if I could meet her in the afternoon. She was in the city anyway, with nothing to do, and she wanted to know me better.

I was overjoyed and we met at a place that was comparable to a diner, located between the dancing school and the train station.

She was wearing an oversized brown pelt coat,

her hair was a mess and her smile was so bright, it blinded me even more than the sunlight reflected in the snow around her.

Once inside, we sat down at a little table that was nothing more than a board mounted onto the wall, with a stool to either side of it. Sitting across one another, we both ordered a warm drink and began talking.

About Rose and how each of us had met her.

About my job and what my expertise was.

About our dancing hobby.

About her relationship to that neighbour boy and how the situation was a bit uncomfortable for her after the breakup.

About my siblings and my relationship to them.

About her permanent fear of being the black sheep in her family, constantly afraid to disappoint her parents.

About our plans for Christmas.

About her love for medieval fairs and a bard she'd met there who had become a dear friend and somewhat of a mentor to her.

About how she had no real friends at school because the boys were all stupid and the girls just children. She needed to talk about the sex she'd had in a car, they needed to talk about some toy or some singer or actress or… whatever.

About the weather and what a mild winter it had been.

About her horse riding hobby.

Our hands intertwined on the table and we soon left to take a walk through the city in the chill, dark winter evening. We found a spot with a stone bench, her standing on top of it to be the same height as me. I told her that her coat looks very snug and comfortable, and she opened it up for me to move my hands inside, wrap my arms around her slim body and share my warmth with hers. We felt each other's heartbeat hammering against our chests and I looked into her eyes for a long silent moment.

I was clearly offering a kiss, and she clearly realized it too, because she giggled and said no, verbally declining my nonverbal offer.

"What *are* we doing here?" She asked this in an amused but sad way, knowing exactly what we were doing but not yet that I was allowed to do it. I took a while to think of an answer and she probably misinterpreted that as me being uncomfortable with the question.

"Want to get back to the dancing school? My training starts in a few minutes." No, I did not want to go back. No, I did not want to relinquish her. But we did. I held her hand as I led her up the stairs and I kissed her forehead to say goodbye.

Then I stayed outside, waiting. For Rose to arrive.

She came, expressed happiness at the surprise, then hugged and kissed me with a warmth that could melt all the snow in the city.

I immediately told her that I had met with Lily in the city. I added that it had been a rather spontaneous thing and I had not had a good opportunity to tell her any earlier.

"I had an inkling that this would happen. Let's talk later."

And then she, too, vanished inside.

When I got home, I already had a few texts from Lily on my phone.

"What were we doing there?"

"What are you trying to do?"

"I really enjoyed this evening."

"I absolutely do not want to hurt Rose."

"I'd love to keep doing this."

"We cannot do this."

Such a perceptive girl. I took my time to reply to her and outlined the rules of my open relationship. I told her about Rose's many exploits. Told her I had not yet slept with anyone other than Rose. Told her I was completely unable to explain to her, in words, what this was that she and I were doing. Reciprocated to her that I, too, wanted to keep doing whatever this was. That we, in fact, could and should keep doing it.

She was overjoyed.

Later that evening, Rose came home, got out of her outside-clothes, looked deep into my eyes and then fired the heaviest ordnances available to her arsenal.

"She's too young. And her ex raped her."

I stood there, unmoving, as my brain slowly comprehended two things.

Rose was going to be my opponent in this.

And Lily urgently needed someone who could show her that love can be something beautiful, something not forced, something that is there when you want and need it and gives you space when you need to be alone. Her soul had wounds that needed mending.

To voice my thoughts it in a modern term, one that is much repeated on the interconnected and vast web: I thought I could fix her.

"I don't want you to get dragged into her mess. Yes, he raped her. He wanted sex, she said no, he did it anyway. And because she was thirteen and dumb, she thought that's what sometimes happens in a relationship. Thought it's normal. You cannot imagine the things I want to do to the fucking arsehole. That's why she's cutting herself. She's in therapy, too."

"I want to keep meeting her. And she wants that, too."

In the moments that followed, she fixed a stare onto me that I still have trouble deciphering. I do believe that the seed of jealousy was already firmly rooted within her, but only in the backdrop of her mind and emotional landscape. At this point, I assume, her thoughts went more into a line of thinking where she wasn't surprised to see me liking Lily, and not surprised to see me ignore all of the red flags she had just waved at me. I am rather convinced that she also felt a queer sort of pride, at me for not abandoning the girl just because I was told to, and at herself for correctly predicting that this would happen. No matter the rails her train of thought passed across though, the station it reached was obvious and clearly stated in further conversation: She expected me, with all this added context, to do the right things, to not do wrong things and to be considerate with the girl at all times. This much, she could rely on. This was the kind of man she was having this relationship with.

And all of these things, I was equally convinced of.

"What do you want with her? Where are you trying to make this go?"

"I only want to enjoy this relationship, this friendship to the fullest. To realize all the interpersonal potential between her and me."

Both of us knew that this meant I wanted to sleep with the girl but that I also would not mind a platonic friendship if that was the maximum attainable outcome.

The major difference between us was, Rose believed that more sex could only be to Lily's detriment and had firm faith in me to not do anything that would harm the girl.

I, on the other hand, was staunchly convinced that sleeping with me would be the best thing that could ever happen to the girl, for she had made bad experiences with bad lovers and someone needed to overwrite this association she had formed by showering her with affection, attention, love and earth-shattering orgasms.

"I say we talk to her next Friday, together, to outline some rules for how this is going to proceed." And with that, Rose was, for the moment, satisfied with the resolution.

The week went by in a flash, with Lily and me frequently chatting through an evening, both anxious to meet on Friday. We each reaffirmed the feelings we had for one another, with her repeatedly saying she would never want to cause trouble for the relationship and me repeatedly reassuring her that this relationship allowed for other people to be in our heart.

When Friday finally came, I asked Rose, in the car, on our way to the dancing school, whether it was okay if I kissed Lily. Rose said she did not mind "if the situation naturally arose." Waiting at the dancing school, I relayed that to Lily, who promptly said "No. I don't want that. What's the worth of a kiss that you had to ask permission for? I'm not doing a planned kiss, that's gross."

Dear reader, as someone who plays games in most of his free time, it is sometimes hard to distinguish real people from NPCs. Mostly, this is the fault of the other person, for being a bland and boring waste of breath, where a superficial glance is sufficient to grasp their full nature and any deeper look reveals nothing of note. In this case, however, the fault lay with me. It was because the situation had been going too well, almost as if it had been scripted. I input attention and affection, and I am getting longing, affection and attention back. As long as I am positive in my communication, the other side was positive as well. The mind of the modern, terminally online man goes into a kind of autopilot, where you say what you think and do what comes to mind without calculating what the realistic response is. Like driving a car. You know those moments where you're fifteen minutes into a drive and cannot remember the last third of the cruise.

It is the same for games and it always happens when things are going comfortably and the next move is rather obvious. If the game is hard and challenging, you sit up straight, fix your posture, check your gear and you go concentrated into that boss fight. If the game is easy, you lean back, rely on your instincts and mechanics and you take every moment as it comes, not thinking much about future repercussions.

I had fallen into the same trap, when sending that text message. If, for a few seconds, I had used my brain capacity there to anticipate her reply, I would have realized sooner the thing that she was outlining as an answer now. Congratulations to myself, we have gotten permission for a kiss. Now we should carefully engineer a situation where it feels natural to actually join our lips to hers, in a hopefully romantic and personal moment underneath the starry sky. She does not need to know about this explicit permission, for we are a trusted partner and would not be doing this if it was not allowed. There is no need, whatsoever, to tell her about this beforehand.

But that is what I had done. The mind had

been on autopilot and seen her as an NPC that dispensed affection when prompted with positive feelings in written or verbal form.

And because I felt a constant urge to talk to her and to get her attention, this had been one more thing to open up a conversation with. Only following this primal impulse, I had not thought past that opener, and thus, not predicted her very predictable reply.

These are not the kind of mistakes I am allowed to make in such a delicate situation. I was in a position where a girl I liked, and especially a girl that I could not even have dreamed of previously, was about to fall in love with me, or had already done so. To ruin this chance, this opportunity, not because of a miscalculation or some deliberate risk I took, but simply because I could not bother to think before acting, that would send me into spiraling despair.

I did not reply to her rebuttal. She was right, after all. What else could I say at this point?

When Lily came into sight, my heart skipped a beat and from the way she smiled at us, I knew she felt the same warmth flooding through her as I did, in that moment. She ran at us with visible excitement, and exchanged a heartfelt embrace with Rose, before getting into a calculated hug with me, that was just a tiny bit shorter than the first one, so as to reassure Rose of her importance in this triangle of relations that was forming between us.

We then took a little walk towards a nearby bakery to sit down with warm drinks and sweet sweets while talking over the important matters. To further reassure Rose of her prominent and important role in the time to come, we walked to her left and her right, giving her the center spot in our middle.

This changed as soon as we entered our destination. We sat down at a small table with a bench on one side and one little chair on the other. I do not remember who sat down in what order, so I am not quite sure who was sending the signal here, but we ended up with me next to Lily on the bench and Rose sitting opposite us. Which accurately represented the sides in the conflict to come.

I put one hand on Lily's left leg, to assuage some of her nervosity and also because I was dying to touch her. She was wearing a thin leggings, appropriate for the dance training in the evening, and I could feel the heat of her body seeping through the fabric, ironically sending shivers down my spine and giving me goosebumps. We already sat close enough to leave no space between us, but she still edged just a tiny bit closer to me in reply to my touch, signaling her approval and enjoyment. It is hard to aptly describe the elation I felt in that moment.

Peace talks soon ensued. Rose took charge, stressing how much she appreciated that two people of such importance to her life were getting along this much. She said she could understand why feelings were developing between the two of us and that she would like to support them. In moderation. She said she was perfectly capable of seeing our body language and the affection shared between us and, pointing out my hand on Lily's leg, how natural these touches already came to us.

At this point, my hand was already slowly working its way away from Lily's knees and towards the center of her body. Moving back and forth, but always ever so slightly more forth, I caressed every inch of her legs that my fingers passed over. The table hid these movements from Rose, who could only roughly tell where my hand was, but not actually observe what was happening.

The reactions I got from Lily fanned the flames of my desire into a scourging inferno. With her hands on the table, holding a warm cup, her ways to communicate encouragement were limited, but she still made sure to use the whole arsenal. There were miniscule movements, increasing the friction between fingers and legs, tiny differences in the pressure her shoulders put into me while leaning on my arm, and she also playfully squeezed my hand between her thighs - until my small finger quested even further upwards, towards the true heat of her body, and she did the opposite of squeezing: She opened up the path.

It was getting harder to listen to Rose, as she expressed support for this burgeoning relationship, told us to mind our limits, not go overboard, listen to one another and to set clear boundaries. She said she would be monitoring the situation, watching how we develop and clearly explained that she retained the right to withdraw all these permissions, at will, to protect her own feelings, or our relationship, or Lily.

Meanwhile, my little finger had found Lily's clitoris and - with movement so miniscule, there was no chance for Rose to catch on - had begun to slowly massage that most sensitive spot through her thin clothes. To this day, I can clearly recall her trying to suppress the little jolts of pressure that I sent through her body. And all the while, she kept her eyes on Rose, nodding, agreeing and giving reassurance that she would stop me if I ever went too far with anything. Which, ironically, I immediately did by applying more pressure, causing her whole body to twitch visibly for a fraction of a heartbeat... But she took it like a warrior, giggled afterwards and hid the true reason from Rose by lying and saying it was a physical reaction, her body expressing the relief felt from gaining Rose's support and permission.

In the end, we all agreed to give this a chance. A hesitant chance, a chance under observation, a chance that could be taken away at a whim. That shining light was still a rising star on the horizon, but it was rising, after all, and I intended to grab it, cherish it, hold it dear and embrace it for as long as I would be granted.

That evening ended on one more high note.

We were walking back through the dark winter evening, this time with me positioned in the middle, holding one hand on each side and smiling from ear to ear. After we reached the dancing school, Rose hugged me goodbye and said she would give us a few minutes alone. She kissed me and went into the building with a wink.

I cannot overstate how much I loved that girl and how happy I was during the seven years of this relationship. I truly think those were the happiest days of my life.

But even happier were the minutes after that door shut behind her.

"What was that?" asked Lily, standing one step higher on the stairs than me, our eyes almost level.

"Are you complaining? You tried very well to hide your enjoyment, but I clearly saw those excited reactions."

"I mean, yes. It was amazing, but…"

She could not say anything more, with my lips

glued onto on hers. I still remember her arms immediately embracing me, pulling me closer, her body greedily taking everything I gave to her in that moment. And we made the moment last, on those stairs and under the stars.

"Now go to your training, Little One. I'll chat you up later. Can't wait to see you again."

"Neither can I."

And so I watched her vanish into that building that I loved so much. I stayed there, in the chill, to contemplate my life, to just enjoy breathing and to think about that past hour. Then I got into my car and drove home.

At the time, Lily was fourteen years old and I was twenty-seven.

"So when we actually do it, I'll do anything you want. I want you to know this. Whatever you tell me to do, I will do."

That was her first message to me, after that amazing evening of permission and our first kiss.

And I was taken aback and shocked at reading this.

Now do not be misguided, I immediately had several fantasies about her that came to mind, some of them less innocent than others. I was very physically attracted to her and I am a person that always flirts with the limits of my partners.

However, my feelings towards Lily always had one counterpart to my carnal greed and my physical hungers, which was - and still is - a strong protective desire. And her saying these things to a man almost twice her age, a man she barely knew yet, a man she had only kissed once... that woke my protective side, even more than it aroused my carnivore instincts.

So I told her that I was flattered, but that this would be an equal partnership. That I might sometimes *ask* things of her, but would never *demand* anything. That she would always be able to stop me, even in the greatest heat of the act. That her well-being would always be the highest priority in this.

You must understand that I still thought I was the thing she needed most.

To this day, I do not know if she was bored by my reassuring side or whether it made her feel safer around me. The years have taught me that she is not just traumatized but utterly broken and she has told me, on multiple occasions, that she likes to feel used. Which goes completely contrary to my love language of caressing and spoiling my partners.

She replied to my explanations and declarations by talking about her fantasies and her past sexual experiences. She wanted to get choked, absolutely did not want to have anal sex again, told me to be rough with her and said that I can bite her wherever the marks wood not be visible.

All these things she wrote and said were so devoid of innocence, it made it impossible for me to consider her a child.

Now I feel, again, the need to defend myself and to give some justification why I felt the right to court her. Had she been untouched, just a sweet girl I knew from my dancing hobby, I would have never dreamed these things about her. Had that hypothetical innocent girl been curious about sex and asked curious questions about the topic to show me that she was interested but not experienced, I would have jokingly told her to find someone she could explore these things with, and that she should stop asking someone like me to give her spoilers about it.

But Lily was not an innocent virgin. And she was absolutely, certainly not going to trust anyone else with her body again any time soon.

I knew I was not taking anything away from her, by showing her the finer points of love, teaching her the arts of the bedroom, by loving her like an adult.

And I knew that no one else would be there for her, simply because she would not let anyone come close to her.

So I replied with some fantasies of my own. Elaborate. Verbose. Detailed.

I wrote her the kind of naughty story that goes on for half an hour and more, nonstop describing how I would caress her body, where I would put my lips, what I would do with my fingers and the things my tongue would do to her… and the protagonists were still far away from the part where anyone takes their pants off.

In life, Lily had not been wearing pants for a while when the little story was finished. It took a few minutes for her to reply afterwards and she then told me this was her first orgasm reached by reading something. She was utterly amazed, asking me to do this more often, and saying she could not wait to do it for real. She then went to sleep, exhausted.

This might seem like I am showing off. And yes, I am cherishing these memories. I will also claim that I am, in fact, good at writing naughty, arousing and engrossing prose. Now I am fully understanding if you find that disgusting or simply find my arrogance insufferable. But I implore you to bear with me. I do not get too many triumphs in this story and it certainly does not end with one.

Which makes these moments all the more valuable and memorable to me.

Now around this time, Rose fell sick. A cold or the flu, something along those lines. She was prone to these things and I rarely managed to handle it the right way. If I doted on her, making tea and lying in bed to keep her warm, she would tell me to get out of the bed because she did not want me to feel bored because of her. If I spent the evening on the computer, she would be annoyed about the lack of attention I showed her.

Accepting that I only had wrong options, I kept her company until she fell asleep, then got up and watched a show that I absolutely hated but wanted to finish so I could complain about it without some twat retorting with a smug "but did you finish it? It gets better later!".

I did not get much watching done.

The age of the Internet is upon us and Lily saw that I was online. Thus began one more evening of talking, joking, flirting and exchanging fantasies. I told her this whole thing felt like an adventure to me, she said she had always hoped to find people like Rose and me in her life and never expected it would actually happen - much less so soon. Before I realized it, midnight had passed. When she finally went to bed, I did the very same, snuggling onto Rose, who snuggled right back into my warm embrace.

"You didn't get much watching done."

"You were awake?"

"Every now and then. But the show was paused every time I snuck a glance."

"I've been writing with Lily."

"I know. Do you want to fuck her?"

This is where every alarm bell in my head should have gone off. They should have screamed a hellish symphony into my head, a crescendoing cacophony urging for caution, a rhythmically ringing chorus imploring me to weigh my every word carefully.

But all that followed her question was silence, inward and outward.

The outward silence, at least, was caused by me thinking about the answer for a bit. Certainly not long or hard enough, but I have to give myself credit for not immediately blurting out something stupid like "yes, I thought that was clear" without considering the possible outcomes of me saying that.

Alas, whether immediate or with pause, that is exactly what I said.

"Yes, I thought that was clear."

I had, once again, been to quick. Too relaxed. Lulled by comfort, my caution dulled by the favorable winds of the journey.

But most importantly, I had been filled with feelings of trust. Or, as I should rather call it with the clarity of hindsight and years of recollection: Faith.

A faith in our relationship.

A faith in Rose, knowing that she would

always come back to me after enjoying someone else.

A faith that she would know the girl is absolutely no threat to her.

A faith that she would also see that I am absolutely no threat to the girl.

A faith that she would see how much this meant to me, how happy this would make me and that it would warm her heart to see me achieve this.

A faith that we had tested the limits of jealousy enough over the course of the last few years for her to be immune to the dangers of that cursed emotion.

As usual, faith, from the perspective of the faithful, is hard to distinguish from knowledge. Especially when said faith had, so far, proved to be correct, outside of a few discrepancies that the faithful faithfully ignore.

Disabusing someone of their faith takes something akin to a miracle. Or, if we are following the analogy correctly, the opposite of a miracle. In a lapse of vocabulary capabilities, I sought to invent a neologism for this, but quickly querying a dictionary reminded me that there are antonyms aplenty already: Disaster. Tragedy. Calamity. Catastrophe.

"She is fourteen years old."

"And you were fifteen. And neither of you innocent at the age."

She mulled over that for a moment, turning

around to face me.

"What do you want, of her? What draws you? What makes her so attractive for you?"

"That is very hard to explain. She is simultaneously vulnerable and assertive. She knows what she wants but knows barely anything about it. She lets me know that she needs me and trusts me. And while I am strongly physically attracted to her, I am equally driven by a desire to answer her needs, to make her happy and to protect her."

"You want to protect her… But aren't your desires exactly the thing she needs protection from?"

"Am I that bad at it?"

"You know that's not what I'm saying."

"I am serious. Am I something people need to be protected from?"

"I… No. You aren't. That is not what I meant and not what I said. It's just that she feels like a little sister to me and I cannot stop seeing her as a child."

"She certainly neither acts nor talks like one with me."

"Yes. With you. Because you have a way to… to extract a side out of a woman that she herself was not even aware of, damn you. I am scared. For her. For us. For you. I'm sorry, I can't consent to sex between you two yet. I hope you understand."

I held her in a warm embrace after that, telling

her how she is the love of my life, telling her I would never leave her, telling her I would never hurt her. I told her I would always respect her wishes and put the relationship first.

Through all this, I felt the tension in her body, and I kept giving her reassurances, kisses to the forehead and gentle touches until she was calm again.

This has always been a relationship built on trust, on understanding one another and on both of us wishing the best for one another. In that moment, my first concern was the stress she was under, for openly opposing me and for stating a taboo that went against the foundation of the open relationship. I knew it had taken her time to come to terms with this herself. Then she'd needed to work up the courage to actually tell me about it. And all this time, she must have predicted hundreds of different reactions from me, some horrible, some devastated, some sad and some angry.

But I loved her. And she was my immediate concern. My only possible reaction was to give her warmth, to praise her for her honesty, to show love and affection, despite her opposition.

Another very important factor to this relationship was honesty.

So when she was calm and comfortable, snuggling into my warm embrace, I spoke up once again.

"You make me happy. I cannot imagine living

without you. I want to grow old with you and raise children with you. I want to come home with a Bernese puppy one day to surprise you, only for you to arrive with a Rottweiler yourself." She giggled when I said that, and the sound still rings true and happy in my ears when I remember it. "I want to nurse you when you're sick, fuck you when you're healthy, hold you when you're tired and dance with you when you're full of energy. I want the two of us to invite our friends to our porch on warm summer evenings and our relatives to hotpot evenings on cold winter nights. I know we will do all these things, and having you in my life makes me feel rich and wealthy."

I then took a break, thinking on my words for once. Feeling her warm breath on my skin, her heart softly beating against my body and the way her hands rested on my back, I certainly hesitated before saying my next thoughts out loud.

"But those are things I have. All of that is part of my life already or certain to be in its future. Lily, right now, is neither certain, nor mine. She has barely entered my life as of now. But of all the things I do not have, all the people not in my life and everything uncertain in this universe, there is nothing I want as much as I want her. Nor will there ever be. So deny this, if you truly must. I will accept that because I love you. But if there is any way for you to allow it, any way at all... please do."

She tightened the embrace and kissed my chest, which was answer enough for me. We spoke no further words before falling asleep each other's arms.

The next week was spent in a strange phase of unclarity.

I wrote to Lily about this new development, explained to her that Rose would, for the moment, not allow the two of us to sleep with one another. Lily was not precisely devastated about it. Her immediate reaction was to look at her calendar and tell me she had no way to spend an evening with me for the foreseeable future anyway, making the point rather moot.

She then, smart as she is, asked me what exactly I meant by saying "for the moment".

As an explanation, I outlined the nightly talks with Rose. Lily, first and foremost concerned with being a bother and a nuisance, as she always felt she was to her own family, apologized for being such a strain on my relationship and wondered if she was damaging her friendship with Rose. I, in turn, told her that Rose was absolutely doting on her and that it was hard to believe that these things could break the bond between the girls, no. Lily then rightfully asked what the reasoning behind the ban might be, if the friendship was as strong as I said it was.

"If I know her correctly, the problem is twofold. For one, jealousy is a difficult beast. It is a real emotion, a physical reaction with a clear source. The first time Rose had slept with another couple, I remember being at home, alone, feeling an unpleasant sensation in my stomach. I have felt jealous before, so the cause was easily identified. But it was lacking the painful emotional punch that usually accompanies the physical feeling. Jealousy, when not accompanied by feelings of betrayal, of insignificance, of uncertainty and grief, loses much of the weight behind its punch. It throws a punch nonetheless. But from my experience, that punch quickly loses its sting, allowing you not only to get used to it, but to ignore it altogether."

"So what do we do?"

"We wait. For her to get used to it. We act like friends towards each other. Touchy friends. Friends who exchange kisses and can't keep their hands off one another. She will grow accustomed to it."

"Are you sure she's fine with that? The touching and the kissing? I don't... I don't want to be a reason for you to fight."

"You aren't. And even if you were, you're worth fighting over."

"Don't say that." I'm sure she was blushing, lying there in the bed of her little room, making lovey dovey eyes at her phone that were meant for me and not for a little rectangle of cold technology.

"So what's the second half of the problem?"

"That she's trying to protect you."

"What? No no no. She doesn't need to, and I don't want that. I'll talk her out of that, just wait. That's not the kind of friendship I want from her. It's the opposite, actually. Didn't you say she's had boys and girls beside you?"

"Yes, she has."

"So she likes girls, too?"

"She sure does."

"I absolutely cannot believe that I found people like you. Do you think we could get her... to join us?"

My heart laughed at that, and I, likewise, could not believe that I found someone like her.

"Let's take small steps first. Get her to accept you and me. Then we take it from there."

"We wanted to meet this week anyway. I'll chat her up."

I have been wrong in my life before. To be precise, I am wrong so frequently that I have had an uncertainty-filled phase where I double checked every decision I made and only outgrew that phase by realizing that my doublechecking was just as flawed and prone to mistakes as my original decisions had been in the first place.

And yet, I cannot remember ever having been as wrong about something before - or ever again - as with my assumption about Rose's tolerance for Lily and I.

Rose grew more annoyed by the day. She must have sent some messages to Lily as well, because Lily, likewise, grew restless and doubtful and hesitant about the whole thing.

I myself was oblivious to this development

and still assumed that we were on track to a new year of happiness and fulfilled desires. I even told Rose that Lily was nurturing doubts and would need some reassuring - optimally coming from her and not me - that all was well and we were still allowed to express our feelings, albeit not in a physically penetrative way.

At this point, I need to explain that I have been the one doing the reassuring, many times before. Since most of Rose's side-boys had been from the friend group or at least acquainted, almost everyone had been hesitant at first, when confronted with the reality that she was interested and making advances towards them. With each and every one of them, I've had "the talk" and made it absolutely clear that she was free to enjoy whomever she liked and that I not only do not harbor any grudges but even encouraged her to live her dreams and desires.

Oblivious about her annoyance and slightly distressed by Lily's growing fears and doubts, I asked Rose to give the girl "the talk" like I had always done with her lovers. I thought she would clear up the situation, answer any open questions and put the limits into clear words to make sure all three of us could be comfortable around one another.

The two went into the city to go shopping, got some cake in a café and just generally had an enjoyable girls' day.

When Rose came home that evening, I waited for a while for her to get settled in, made her laugh with some joke and then asked her how her day had been.

She said it had been very enjoyable and talked about the fun things they'd done, the places they'd been and the things they had seen.

I then asked her how the talks about me had gone.

"Oh sorry. We were so occupied that you didn't even come up as a topic."

I did not have the heart to be angry with her. I told myself that I should have known she would not clear things up.

Not because I knew her heart, no. I was still utterly convinced that she could never betray my trust and, after all the freedom she had enjoyed in this relationship, deny me this one thing I wanted most. The astute reader might have realized by now, that this trust was unfounded and this dream-castle of mine was built on pillars of salt and pillars of sand, to quote a song that I am very fond of.

No, in my boundless arrogance, I attributed this failure to her overall predisposition for incompetence.

This may sound harsh, but I will give some examples.

Rose was the kind of person that would drop her phone in the sink while doing the dishes.

She frequently hit me with her knees when climbing over me in bed. This happened so much, in fact, that I always made sure to have "my spot" on the wall-side of the bed, to minimize situations where any climbing was necessary.

At a summer festival in town, she introduced one of our friends to her friend group but gave an entirely wrong name because she just had too many thoughts in her head at the same time and jumbled them together in that moment.

A feud at the dancing school began with her

ramming a car door into the car next to us.

It is not possible to count the amount of times she ran into my bookshelf or my dumbbells at home and we rarely ever spent a day together without her frantically searching for her phone at some point.

I cannot even claim that she attracted disaster. But she usually made no attempts at avoiding it either.

All this, I do not lay at her feet as blame. These things made her more endearing, if anything, and I had made it a habit to look out for things she could hurt herself or others on.

The reason why I list these things, why I outline this trait of hers in such detail is because I need to explain why I still did not suspect any malice in her actions.

Instead of doubting her support for this blossoming relationship with Lily, I attributed her failing assistance to her sheer general inability to do things correctly.

A new Star Wars movie came to theaters around this time. I had asked some friends to go the theater together and we had set a date on one fateful Friday evening. With Rose's permission, I had also asked Lily to join us.

She said that she had never seen a Star Wars movie before, but it sounded like a fun day and she would be happy to see us again. Only, she had dancing lessons around noon and would need a way to pass the time until the start of the movie. I offered to pick her up so she could stay at my place. Rose approved this course of action.

As this Friday grew closer, Rose grew more restless, still watching me throw heart-shaped glances at my phone whenever Lily sent a message.

And one evening her emotions just exploded out of her.

"She is *fourteen*!"

"Yes. We have been over this. You were fifteen."

"But this is different. She's a child!"

"So were you. And here we are, five happy years later."

"You do not understand. I can't watch this any more."

She rummaged around in one of the chests that harbored an assortment of things that had no real home in my flat but still needed a spot where she could put them. I groaned when she came back with the little notebook that outlined the rules of our relationship and skimmed the pages for a bit.

"I'm adding an age minimum. No partners below the age of sixteen."

"Sensible. It's not like I'm specifically targeting those anyway. But you do realize that there is no way for me to accept that we are adding rules after the fact and then retroactively applying them to things that are already in full swing?"

"Oh, in full swing, are we? What are you swinging towards? You just want to fuck her, don't you?"

"You know that's not true. I just feel so much appreciation and admiration towards her - and from her - and I want to live all of it without restraints. That's what this was always about. A way for us to make sure we never see this relationship as something that impedes us, and rather as something that fuels us, supports us and allows us to live our dreams."

"So you don't want to fuck her?"

"That's not what I said. If the situation naturally arises, I sure won't deny her."

"Naturally." She spat that word out with such venom. "Oh I know your nature and hers well enough to see that it's unavoidable. And it makes me sick. You made her fall for you with your weird irresistible charisma and your magic words and now you're claiming shared blame because she also wants you and this is somehow happening on its own."

"She's wanted me from the first time she's talked to me. I am flattered by your allegations of magic, but even if I were capable of such sorcery, the spell was wrought before I even knew she existed."

"And that is the only reason I watched this and tolerated it so far." A deep exasperated sigh. "What if you were caught? Did you ever give that any thought?"

"No, I didn't. Same way you never worry about your parents finding out how many of our friends you've ridden. Neither of us are stupid enough to let these things come to light."

"But you can never be sure! Secrets get out. You say you want to protect her, but you are opening her up to this risk…"

"Yes, and you want to protect her by depriving her of the one source of happiness she has right now. That's even more of a risk, considering her tendency to hurt herself. The alternative to her being with me is her getting together with some guy from her school or her village who clumsily uses her as a sex object for a few weeks until he moves on to the next girl he needs to indifferently plough." I hesitated for a bit, because the next part would upset her. "Don't pull the brakes on us now. I can't stop you. But you will deal so much damage. To her. To your friendship with her. And I hate to say it, but this will drive a wedge between you and me that I cannot mitigate."

"Yes. Because I'm always such a bother to you." She was close to tears there, angry, sad, disappointed and confused… My heart burst with compassion, but I could not surrender here.

"You're not. I love you and I will always choose you over anyone else. But I am desperately begging you not to ask it of me."

"She's not just a sex object to you?"

"No. She's a friend. She's someone to admire. Someone who admires me. Someone I want to cherish and spoil, guard and protect."

She sniffled, then embraced me.

"I'm just so scared. This whole thing, I never wanted this. I just…"

"Don't be. I'll protect you too. Like I always have."

And with that, I kissed her forehead, full of unconditional love.

Cinema day had come. Rose had university that day and would meet with one of her other boys in the afternoon, who would also watch the movie with us.

I drove to the dancing school in the early afternoon and while some things of this day remain in my memory like crystal clear photographs, others have completely faded. I can not tell you which car I was driving at the time, although that could be looked up. I have no memory of the weather that day. I would remember it, of course, had it been memorable. So let us assume a cloudy and mildly cold winter day.

Imagine me restlessly pacing back and forth among the grey concrete pillars of our dancing school's parking lot. That utterly unromantic place had ironically been the setting for many a romantic conversation over the years, and I assume that I am not the only one with many fond and some very un-fond memories rooted there.

This would be one of the fonder ones, despite the sight of her damnable shadow at her side as Lily came down the stairs. Packed into her brown winter coat, she looked small next to her detestable dance partner, who, in turn, probably looked small next to me. At the time, I did not have such burning hatred for him yet, but the man was always slightly unsettling in his posture, behavior and his facial expressions.

What I knew about him at the time made me scorn him, but I had not yet fantasized about murdering him.

"Ah. Hi. Did you also have training today?"

"No. He's here to pick me up. I told you, you don't have to drive me home today."

He looked rather lost, hearing that. I had always assumed him to be very stupid, but I'd never wasted enough time listening to him to verify the theory before.

"So, uh, you're going…"

"We're watching the new Star Wars." I was the picture of politeness, and, feeling an absolute sense of superiority over him, even decided to show some generosity. "You could come with us, if you'd like."

Of course, I only said that because I was very sure he would decline it. Even if he didn't, I'd merely tell him the time for the movie and not offer to entertain him in the hours between.

"No, thank you. I don't watch that kind of movie." I'd love to call him an arrogant bastard for that, but it was a movie from the awful trilogy, and his disdain, while rooted in entirely the wrong reasons, was warranted. I myself only wanted to see it out of a sense of completionism and because it was a nice way to spend a day with friends.

"Alright then, see you around."

I gave a quick hug to Lily as a greeting. No kiss this time, considering the company. We left

off, towards my car and when I piloted the
vehicle out of the parking lot, the dumb fellow
still stood there, as if he had to contemplate
what just happened before he could move on to
his own automobile.

Lily held my hand all the way back to my flat.

"Why would you ever invite him? What was
that?"

"I was very sure he'd decline. And it sends a
message that we're not going to do anything he
wouldn't approve of."

"Oh, but we are!" The grin she gave me in that
moment will forever burn in my heart.

As soon as we entered my flat, she got rid of
her coat and threw herself against me, burying
her face into my chest. I stood there, holding her,
in front of my wardrobe mirror, just holding her
until I felt some of the pressure subside. I then
softly nudged her chin with my hand so she
would face me and we exchanged one
passionate and hungry kiss, long overdue and
still much too short.

"Don't you want to do this on the bed?"

It was her, who said that. Gods be good.

Some of you may want to skip this chapter.

I thought long and hard about whether I would even include the details of that day. But if George R.R. Martin can write all those scenes about 13 years old Daenerys and still sell millions of books, I should be on the safe side writing about the few hours Lily and I spent in my bed.

Still, the chapter will be physical and explicit. You will miss nothing of the story if you stop here and continue at the next chapter.

I needed no second invitation to throw her onto the bed and jump after her. Resting my weight on my hands, I held myself above her and looked down into those amazing eyes staring back at me. There was so much emotion in that face, ranging from excitement, to a bit of worry and hesitation, but also so much trust and, undeniably, love. Eager to erase every negative experience she had ever had with men, I moved closer and began by overwriting her memories of kissing. Her eyes closed before our lips touched. Her hands closed around my back as I playfully rubbed my nose against hers. I felt a shudder go through her whole body when my mouth finally found Lily's and it felt like my mind and body were melting under the heat of that contact.

She dug her fingers into my hair, keeping my head right where it was and not allowing me to interrupt this kiss until she herself decided she was finished with it. We held that embrace, that blissful moment for minutes, drinking deep from the well of happiness and filling our brain with emotions that no one else could provide. When she finally let go of my head, I shifted my weight slightly to get even more physical contact with her and instead of ending the kiss only made it more intense. The last signal I wanted to send was that I only kissed her as long as she made me do it. When I parted my lips to get a bit more invasive, she gently disentangled our faces from each other.

"No tongue, please. Not yet."

"Not there, at least." I gave a raspy laugh and ran it across her neck and shoulders instead, tasting and feeling her goosebumps, then digging my teeth into the soft flesh right above her collarbone. Had I recorded the moan that escaped her in that moment, I would still be replaying it every day. There are men who have had decades of sex and still never got to hear such a sound of release and relief, excitement and ecstasy even once. She was intoxicating. My mind was already swimming and we had barely begun.

Kissing her again, I moved myself off her body to free up my hands and moved one of them underneath her pullover to gently caress that flawless skin of her stomach. I felt her shiver again and she turned towards me to face me and resume kissing. My fingers traveled up and down her sides, from hip to armpit and back, sometimes softly and sometimes with a bit of fingernail teasing quick breaths and soft moans out of her.

She spoke up, the next moment she had enough breath for it and we weren't locked into a kiss.

"I know you want to touch them. Go do it!"

When my hand slid up her body again, I moved it to cup one of her breasts. She was very sensitive even through her bra, throwing her head back in enjoyment and moving her chest even closer to me. Surprised by their size, I broke character for a moment, my hand switching from caressing movement to a more quizzical and explorative questing. She quickly noticed the change, then saw my puzzled expression and raised an amused eyebrow.

"That's a lot more than I expected. Those pullovers are hiding treasure underneath."

She giggled and got on top of me.

"Time to unearth that treasure for you."

I still see the rays of sunlight outlining her body on top of mine, as she took the lower end of her sweater into her hands and pulled it over her head. The movement of her arms was mesmerizing, her smooth stomach stunningly beautiful and the way you could just about guess the contours of her ribs when she stretched her body will forever be ingrained into my brain. She threw the piece of clothing on the floor and shook her head, throwing her short dark locks into every direction, then saw my look of utter amazement and let out a laugh that could make a dying man smile.

"So you like what you see?"

"I absolutely fucking love it."

I sat up, trying to take her whole body into my hands, running them from her hips across her back until it was me who grabbed her head and pressed her into a kiss. Slowly pulling her down with me, we resumed that long, passionate embrace from the beginning, except now it was me on my back and her above me. I felt her hips rubbing against mine and when I finally let go of her head, she got upright, moved her weight a bit and searched for that bulge in my pants by slowly moving her hips back and forth.

The moment she found it, she put her weight into that point of contact and changed rhythm to an absolutely ecstatic experience.

I cannot describe the feeling of a girl riding you that spent years in the stable and the dancing studio. Moving their hips comes as naturally to them as flying comes to a bird and she soared in that moment, giving herself entirely to that pressure between her legs, every movement maximizing the pleasure she got from it. It is a miracle I did not have an orgasm right then and there.

When she finally took an exhausted break, I

gently moved her next to me, invaded her pants with my left hand and started massaging her through her underwear, right at the clitoris, providing a pleasure far more intense than her own riding had yielded.

"Why are we" she panted "even doing this" a moan "when we're not allowed to fuck?"

"Because we want to." I kissed her lips. "Because it's fun." I kissed her neck. "You can't tell me you're not enjoying this." I took her nipple between my lips and applied pressure, still working with my hand between her legs.

"But it's soo frustrating. How do you deal with the disappointment of having to stop here?"

"It is far outweighed by the triumph of getting this far." I kissed her lips again, sending shiver upon shiver across her body with every tiny movement of my fingers now accustomed to her and perfectly placed to elicit these reactions. "And I have to admit, I am finding myself more and more indifferent to Rose's taboos."

"You want to…" I kissed her again.

"I'm not sure yet. But I don't think I'll be able to stop if this keeps going."

She got back up, kissing my neck and pulling my shirt up to kiss my chest, still sitting on that hand, with my fingers still moving against her underwear.

"I'm sorry, but I'm bleeding today. Too much for sex. Honestly, I absolutely do not know how you are doing all this despite my body violently ejecting any ideas of having sex today. *He* never managed to get me horny on my period." She pulled my hand out of her pants and got on top of me to ride me again, wild and greedy, her hips barely controlled but still with amazing technique. I drank that view in, swearing to never forget a single movement of her body.

Part of me was glad about her period, because it saved me from breaking Rose's taboo. Then again, the knowledge, the certainty that I would have broken it that day… That already counts as cheating to me. And I will be forever ashamed of myself for that. The parts of me that aren't glad about her period do of course hate every deity, every god and every cosmic being that could be held accountable for making her bleed on that day, of all days.

When Lily was exhausted again, lying next to me and looking at me with those eyes high on love and happiness, I suggested she move her hand into my pants this time.

"I'm not sure."

"You really want to miss that? You already somewhat know what awaits you. I know you're curious to meet him."

She gave me that look that I knew from Rose. That look that says "how does he do this?"

Then her hand moved across my chest, making sure to stop after every single rib before crossing over my stomach, circling my bellybutton and then moving even further down. I gave her a kiss and also moved my lips down, applying pressure to her nipple again, but using my teeth this time. She moaned, fiddled with my pants and then she was in, grabbing hold of my throbbing penis.

"You were not kidding when you said I'd need two hands for this one."

Her hand moved up and down the length, then grabbed me with such confidence and began stroking it with such experienced movement that I could not help a pang of sadness at being physically confronted with the fact that she had a sexual past already.

I still know that this was our exact position, her hand stroking my dick and my teeth working on her nipple, both of us still wearing pants, when my best friend knocked at my door, here to pick us up for the movie.

For those who skipped it, there is one key detail in the last chapter that still haunts my conscience from time to time.

We did not have sex, because she was on her period. But that was the only thing holding us back. I was ready to cheat on Rose and despite not doing it, that counts as cheating, at least in my mind.

But rest your mind, no innocent maidens were penetrated in that skipped chapter. Partly because she was nowhere near innocent. Chiefly because I did not penetrate her.

I rarely ever disliked the arrival of my best friend to any occasion.

We will call him Atlan, because he called himself that when we were still gaming almost daily in our teenage years.

Atlan and I first met when we were five and six years old respectively. We spent most of our childhood together. We lived together in a flat for years after we'd both graduated. I almost cried when he told me his dog died. If I ever find a woman to marry, he will be my best man at the wedding.

And yet, when he knocked on my door that day, violently ripping Lily and me out of our blissfully erotic afternoon, I could have strangled him.

No fault of his, of course. We were scheduled for him to pick us up, after all, and he was right on time - while ours had run out. For a moment, I seriously thought I should send my friends on ahead without us and move things with Lily into the shower, where her blood would maybe pose as less of an inhibition. But I am not completely insane and I discarded that idea just as quickly as I had come up with it.

I yelled through the door that he should take the other entrance, of course not explaining to him that Lily and I needed the time to get dressed and at least fix some of our appearance to not look like we'd just spent hours copulating like rabbits.

We certainly managed to get dressed, but I assume we thoroughly failed the appearance part, for Atlan and my roommate both had that look on their face when they saw us that screams "he cannot be serious."

They said nothing, thankfully. Lily and I got onto the backseats of the car and I do not know whether she wanted more of my attention or if she noticed the distaste my friends felt at her presence, but she reached out for my hand, and I held and squeezed it to give her all the comfort I could with that little gesture.

Rose was already at the movie theater when we arrived, sitting next to a lover of hers who was coincidentally my roommate's brother. We were one tight-knit bunch.

With that lover to her left, there was only one

spot to sit next to Rose. Clearly, there are two ways to sit. Lily could sit next to her, placing her in the middle between Rose and me. That would fit the whole idea of being protective for her. Guarding her from left and right, together. On the other hand, I could sit next to Rose myself, projecting that I was still close to her and that nothing was pushing us apart. So we stood there, in front of those two free seats, and I kept wondering what the better setup could be. I was hoping for Rose to give me a sign, but I do not think she recognized my conundrum.

Eventually, I directly asked her who to should sit next to her.

"You. No, wait. Let Lily sit between us. Yes, thank you."

When everyone was seated and the lights were dimmed, I put my hand on Lily's leg and she immediately grabbed it, not letting go for the entirety of the movie.

The next few hours provided a multitude of different stages of displeasure for everyone involved.

Most of our group felt a mild discomfort at Lily being there. Except for Rose, who felt a mixture of happy, because she was a good friend. and horrible, because she had instantly noticed a change in our chemistry when we had entered the room. Lily and I, of course, were thrilled by each other's company, but the way we held hands on her leg only contributed to

Rose's woes.

The movie itself was also very displeasing. I have said before that this was a movie from the awful trilogy, and the writing was devoid of any intelligence. I should have left the cinema in protest, but then I would have had to watch it again at a later date, so I could complain about it without some twat saying "but did you watch the whole thing? The finale was grand!" I do believe we have already established this earlier with either books or some show: I finish bad fiction so that I am qualified to verbally vomit about it afterwards. In any case, everyone from our group had this adding to his discomfort.

But there was one other thing that ruined the already strained mood for each and every one of us.

Near the midpoint of the movie, Rose got up and stormed out of the theater.

A smart man would have chased after her.

I am not a smart man. I believe that much has been gotten across to the reader in the story so far.

I stayed in my seat, partly because I wanted to get this movie over with, partly because I did not want to leave Lily alone, who was already very uncomfortable with the situation and mostly because I really did not want to be confronted with Rose's tantrum.

So I stayed, enduring the entire movie. Afterwards, we all drove to our place together to have somewhat of an afterparty in my roommate's room, with beer, music and maybe some fun videos on his projector.

Rose, who had not said a word after the leaving the cinema finally spoke up to say that it was probably for the best to drive Lily home immediately. No one dared object and we swapped over to my car, Rose riding shotgun and Lily in the back. All three of us remained silent throughout the trip.

"Wait in the car, dear."

I was a dear and waited. Said goodbye to Lily and watched the two people I loved most in the world walk to that village house with the big yard, the small fence and the massive glass front and I watched them vanish behind that door on the first floor.

And then I waited for that door to open again. It took a bit over half an hour until Rose came back out, alone. She got into the car, looked at me and gave one exasperated sigh.

"It's done. I ended it. Please just get us home."

I was remarkably calm, driving us home. Concentrated on the road and the steering wheel, I kept my thoughts to myself just as Rose did, sitting next to me.

The assumption is, of course, that she was simultaneously angry at me for everything that had happened, relieved that it was now over and also somewhat scared of my reaction, which was sure to come out at some point.

But I was tranquil. There was no pent-up anger brewing inside me, no wrath waiting to explode out of the pot's lid.

Clearly, my mind was telling me, this whole thing had been too good to be true. How silly of me, to actually expect this to work out. This was not a downfall, it was a return to normalcy.

Over the course of the twenty minutes it took us to get home, I managed to convince myself that this was nothing to be angry over.

Rose had always been, and still was, the love of my life. Lily would have only been a bonus. A very nice bonus, an ecstatic and euphoric bonus, but I still had the one thing that made me happy in this life.

There was no way that fate would have allowed me to just win at life, to get what I wanted most and be even happier than I already was. After all, it had been a miracle for me to even be allowed this current degree of happiness.

Furthermore, I should have known that Rose

destroys anything she touches, after all. I had known this habit of hers for years and still loved her thoroughly, after all. I put this whole thing into her destructive hands, after all. Feigning trust where I should not have had any. After all, I never hand her anything we might still need. So was it stupidity, giving her a chance to break this? Or was it destiny, fate, preordained? No, I am not a religious or superstitious man.

Neglect or oversight had nothing to do with it. Nor any higher powers, meddling in our pithy lives. No, it had been my own subconscious decision, that ruined this. I allowed her to destroy this, because I needed her to. Because, somehow, I had known that this could not be.

As you can see, my brain was desperately trying an Olympiad's worth of mental gymnastics to find a way not to hate Rose. I managed to pin the blame onto myself, to pull it away from her, to not associate her with something that stands in my way and turns my dreams into ashes with a foul touch.

This was only met with partial success.

I absolutely managed to direct some of my hate towards myself, to ruin any appreciation I had for my own person. This would be a rather consistent part of my life, from here on out. A feeling that nothing would ever get better. That this was as good as it gets. That I did not deserve, and thus would never achieve more than I already had. That my life had peaked, on that afternoon in my bed, with a pleasure I stole from the universe the same way Prometheus stole the flame and that I was henceforth cursed to have my heart eaten, not by some bird of prey, but by little insect-like avatars of doubt, mistrust and resignation.

The thing I failed to do, in increasing the loathing I felt for myself, was to shield Rose from it. I still loved her, and that love outweighed any possible negative emotions for her. But I had never really felt any negative emotions towards her before, except for a bit of disdain for her clumsy tendencies. But now, for the first time in my life, I felt vindictive towards her. I vowed to deny her something, something big, something she really wanted, something life changing at some point in the future, in reply to what she had done today.

This was another mental trick I played on myself. By focusing any vengeful feelings, which I undoubtedly had in spades that evening, towards an undefined point in the future where I could pay her back in full, I made it possible for myself not to do anything stupid in the moment and in our day to day life.

When the car was parked and the thinking was done, I had resolved myself to close this chapter of my life, to not mourn it and to keep enjoying what I had, instead of longing for what could not be.

One of my best friends, you might remember Diego, used to say "you can't always have what you want. But you can always want what you have."

I suppose he's not saying that any more, but at the time of our story, he still had this mantra guide his life and I supposed that I might take a leaf from his book.

"Can we agree to never talk about this again? It's over and done with."

"I'd prefer that, yes. I'm just happy I was able to stop it before anything serious could happen."

I never even asked her - or Lily, for that matter - what exactly they had told one another in that long talk behind Lily's home door.

No, instead of asking that one important thing, that question that has now haunted me for years, I threw all my resolve out of the window straight away and said the most offensive thing that could come to my mind.

"I just hope you gave her some time to wash her hands. My sperm must have felt uncomfortably sticky this whole evening."

I used the following weeks to constantly tease Rose with little allusions to my almost-affair. While I cannot deny that I derived some sadistic pleasure from it, the intent was not even malicious.

On one hand it really helped me. Whenever something bothers me, I cope by talking about it. And you have guessed correctly, me sitting here and writing this book is one example of that.

On the other hand, it has been hard for me, my whole life long, to not tell a joke once I had conceived it. This has cost me a handful dates in the past and over the course of our relationship, I'd had to realize that Rose really did not appreciate some of my more controversial humor either.

So in the immediate phase after Rose broke Lily and me up, I simply lost the usual inhibition that I had acquired around her, going back to my natural state of speaking my humorous mind, no matter who could feel offended by it.

I do think an example is in order.

As the birth of Christ finally came around (yes, the story this far was completely contained in the first three weeks of that December), my parents invited us to a cozy Christmas fair at a local farm, a location that was well known in the area because of this one yearly event. We had a very wholesome evening there, surrounded by old barns, newborn lambs, well-done pork and with lots of sweetened hot wine to drink. We stood around a fire in a barrel, walked between stands selling accessories or sweets and I warmed Rose's hands by taking them into mine. I caught up with my father about his new retirement plan and my brother searched the shops for a specific item with my mother.

In one of the stables, there was a petting zoo and and Rose was allowed to feed one of the infant goats and ruffle its fur. An adorable scene, with her yelping every time the animal's rough tongue touched her hand and swooning about how sturdy the hairs on that horned little head had felt.

"So why are you allowed to put seed into something young and cute and I'm not?"

That put her close to tears, which definitely overshot my intentions. Luckily for me, she had no one else to seek comfort with, so she put those glistening eyes towards me, clearly indicating that she needed someone to hold her, even if it was the person that made her feel sad in the first place.

She did not cry, with her face pressed into my shoulder. But I heard a muffled "fuck you", which made me laugh, kiss her forehead and pull her closer towards me.

"I know you need this. Truth be told, it would be scary if you didn't show your anger at all. I'd be terrified if you bottled it up. But please. Leave it at this one for today, yes?"

"You know I could never hate you. But I hate

what you did. And I need to slowly work that off. Still, I promise I'm done for today."

That evening is among the fondest memories I have, not just of that relationship, but of my life. We shared a bag of roasted almonds, laughed at wooden boards displaying silly provincial proverbs, we toasted to the coming year with my family and we found a bale of hay to cuddle on, under a starlit sky.

Lily and I were still writing. With Rose not at all elaborating on any new rules other than "it's over now", we made our own rules, which were, as you might guess, rather lenient. We kept flirting and we even did some more sexting, prompted by Lily asking me what I'd do if we were allowed to.

But soft as our breakup may have been, she absolutely did not take it well. Which is understandable, considering how bad I was taking it - while still having a girlfriend to comfort me. She had no one.

While I used dumb and offensive jokes to cope, Lily went back to scarring her arms and even extended her self harming to her legs.

"I can understand Rose's point, really. She's right. But still, losing this, losing you... It hurts. It just hurts so much. I feel so empty right now, not knowing why I even get up in the mornings. Christmas evening with the family was horrible and I locked myself into my room after dinner."

"That sounds so sad to me. My family has always been a retreat, a refuge, a place of love and warmth to me. I wish you could also fall back on that."

"I'd love that. I hoped you could be that for me… Now the only warmth I get is from this bath I'm in. It's kinda hard to decide between drowning myself, shaving my leg or opening my veins underwater."

"You're bathing? I'd love to be there. What are you wearing?"

"Nothing, idiot. Here, look." She sent a picture of her leg. Knee and upper thigh were protruding through the foaming water, the rest of her body was hidden below all the soap bubbles floating on the surface.

Our chat remained a source of comfort for one another and it stayed somewhat flirty and romantic, but it was now a far cry from the heat and intensity that had defined it previously. It certainly was not enough for her to cope with her assaulted past, her awful family situation and our recent shared disappointment adding to her depressions.

We did agree on continuing this friendship, both unable to cut the other out of their life. We both resolved not meet one another, while emotionally in the state we found ourselves in - for we knew we would break any rules once left alone in a room together. And, despite me not at all believing that her feelings could last that long, we both promised one another to resume our romance in 18 months, on the day of her sixteenth birthday.

I later used that bathtub picture for another jab at Rose.

One evening, I asked her what the dinner plan was and she talked about throwing some noodles and vegetables into a pan, with some sauce to season it. I then showed her that photo and said that this looked even tastier and whether I could have that instead.

She did get very angry at that one, which led to me eating bread that evening and to her calling Lily to reprimand her. "You can't send him stuff like that. We talked about this."

Please understand, dear reader, that this was part of our relationship. Honesty dictates that I was always going to show that picture to her. I simply did it in a way that helped me deal with my emotions.

One week into January, I got up in the evening and took a look at my phone to find four messages from Lily. Four deleted messages. The device only told me they had arrived twenty minutes ago and been retracted shortly after that.

Immediately fearing that she might have hurt herself, I wrote back and asked if everything was okay and whether she needed my help. For reasons I cannot explain and do not understand myself, it did not cross my mind to call her. Instead, I sat there, in the dark, only illuminated by the light from my screen and praying to no one in particular for her to reply. The seconds stretched into eternities, with me sweating profusely and dreading the worst until finally three dots blinked up before my eyes.

"Sorry, can't talk. On the way to the hospital."

And with that, she was out of reach for the foreseeable future.

Terrified of her own urges to self-harm and more importantly her strong desire to kill herself, she no longer felt safe at home, unsupervised in her small, dark and stuffy room…

Her solution was as saddening as it was effective. She cut herself so deeply, her parents were forced to drive her to the hospital and, after being sent to a youth psychologist and opening up about her problems, the hospital, in turn, had no choice but to take her in for a supervised stay.

The policies of the youth psych ward allow visits exclusively from family members, if at all. Another step taken by the hospital staff is to take away all electronic devices of communication. Considering the kinds of trauma sustained by their patients and the fact that most of them were inflicted by someone who may or may not still play a role in their life, these measures appear prudent to me and are more than understandable.

But no amount of understanding could help with the fact that I missed her horribly. I had already been unable to see her, of course, but to have her physically locked away made it even worse, especially because I knew that I had failed her by not seeing those four messages in time. Maybe I could have prevented this. Maybe they were a call for help. I will never know.

Then, to add doubts and fears to my commencing misery, I constantly dreaded that I myself might get locked out of her heart now, for time has proved again and again to be ever the enemy of passion.

I must, at this juncture of our retelling, come back to that saying I quoted previously. That one mantra my dear friend Diego used to swear on. I will repeat it here to spare you the effort of leafing back to find the exact passage:

"You cannot have everything you want. But you can want everything you have."

The astute reader will have realized that I have not once in my life believed this to be true and that I, unlike my dear friend who at least tried to base his life on this for many years, have consistently showed disdain for this particular school of thought through my actions.

I rather ascribe to an entirely different, and altogether shorter and much simpler maxim:

"Enjoy life as much as possible!"

Whenever you are unhappy, seek that which makes you happy. Whenever you are happy, seek that which either gives you a permanent greater happiness or fleeting moments of complete bliss.

What does not work for me is to be content. I am unable to want what I already have, and the English language supports my argument in this case, for he who is lacking something essential is "found wanting".

One time, Diego and I had a long philosophical debate about these conflicting views. In the end, we both appeased the other by admitting some merits in his approach to life, but each of us stressed how he would still stay true to his own belief and was far from convinced of the other's point.

This has been somewhat of a tangent, and it turned out longer than initially intended, which does not bode well for my next point. For whenever I go on these elaborate tangents, it is to prime and prepare the reader, to set a groundwork upon which my next actions or decisions can be explained. Applying this knowledge, we can use the length of the premeditated excuses to make approximations about how dumb and stupid said actions and decisions are going to be.

Rest assured, I gave Lily all the distance warranted by law, love and common sense.

But instead of fixing the cracks that Rose and I had just opened up in my existing relationship, which is something I already had and could not want, I put absolutely no focus onto Rose and instead began a new romance with a girl we shall henceforth call Dandelion.

Dandelion was another girl from our dancing school, one that had a meteoric rise through the tournament ranks.

And she has always had an obvious crush on me.

Every time she saw me arrive at a party, she jumped, hopped and skipped to me with a giddy giggle, asking "is Rose with you today?" with the biggest grin on her face... which always faded because I consistently answered with a yes.

Nomen est omen, as roman playwright Plautus so aptly put it, thousands of years ago (I must admit that I looked up the origin of this idiom one minute prior to starting on this chapter. I am by far not as well-read and educated as I try to seem to the eyes of an untrained reader). In Dandelion's case, I choose this pseudonym for her because she was young and green, a beautiful flower with a golden mane on her head and... the longer you know her the more you realize what an airhead she is.

As an innocent virgin and a sheltered princess, the concepts of an open relationship, polygamy and emotional frustrations were entirely alien to her. To be precise, she saw the topic of relationships itself as foreign and only tried to understand it from the point of an outsider.

To her, it was set in stone that a person with a girlfriend is off-limits to anyone else. You were either taken or not taken. She did not comprehend that there were   obviously steps inbetween that, like phases where you are getting to know one another but not yet committed, nor did it ever cross her mind that there were different kinds of couples with individualized sets of rules between them.

So whenever I tried to reciprocate some of these feelings she harbored for me which she so utterly failed to hide from the public, she always declined, for fear of intruding and because she simply thought that there was no point to meeting a man she was in love with, if he already loved someone else.

Still, I asked her out on a date every few months, which had become somewhat of a running joke for me, a reason to chuckle to myself every time she conjured some convoluted excuse to decline without ever giving an appearance that she was not interested in me. I can picture the anxiety she felt, always dreading that she might say something wrong and make me feel unwanted or even insulted.

Imagine my surprise when, in early spring of the new year, I asked her out on a date again, partly out of habit and partly because I needed some way to take my mind off the Lily disaster - which was still eating away at my brain like a termite colony crunching through the roof beams of grandma's garden hut - and Dandelion happily agreed and said she was looking forward to it.

At first we had to postpone by one day, from a Friday to a Saturday, purportedly because she was visiting her grandparents on Friday.

When Saturday finally came around, she rode her bicycle to my flat and we spent a beautiful and sunny afternoon in the city. We enjoyed sweet and flavorful ice cream while walking alongside a sparkling canal in the centuries-old center of the town, then went to one of my favorite green parks and lounged around on the cut grass. Wholly unprepared, we had brought no blanket nor picnic rug to lie on, but we sat on the lawn anyway, engaged in an engrossing conversation about nothing at all.

I can say, without exaggeration, that I do not remember a word of what we talked about. What I do remember is the way her almost bare legs kept distracting me while she was laying on her belly next to me, wagging her feet in excitement just like the dogs around us were wagging their tails. Any other position would have been less revealing and less eye-catching, but with the beginning of the warmer seasons, she had decided to wear trousers today, that, while too long for a warm summer day, still allowed for air circulation because their bottom half was cut open on the backside, just like some dresses are cut open at the side.

Lying face-down, her lower legs were completely in the open, presenting the well trained calves of a successful dancer, with the caramel complexion only achieved by being a non-pale, blond girl who spends a lot of time in the sun. At one point, I interrupted myself mid-sentence to bend over and kiss that part of her legs, claiming that it would have been impossible to focus on the conversation without getting that intrusive thought out of my brain. She giggled and blushed and the old man sitting on a bench nearby gave a hearty laugh, entertained by my sheer audacity.

I remember us rolling through the grass multiple times that afternoon, in order to stay ahead of the moving shadows thrown by the ancient government buildings surrounding the greenery. Eventually, there were no sunny spots left at all, prompting a change of location. We walked, hand in hand, to a small Indian-operated food establishment near my flat which I refuse to call a restaurant. The place sold curry and rice based dishes as you would expect and associate with the nationality and identity presented, but also had some sort of corporate contract with some sort of nameless and faceless fast food corporation, for you could opt to buy pizza or burgers or fries there. The shop was small enough to be overfilled with more than three customers present and - with all due respect and no racism at all intended - smelled exactly the way you would expect from a permanently heated place suffused in the sweat of three Indian workers, mixed with the fumes of frying oil and all sorts of curry related seasoning.

I wanted to spare Dandelion the malodorous experience and went inside on my own, but the man operating the establishment was clearly even more confused by my companion's order than I had been, a minute earlier. She wanted butter chicken, but as a vegetarian she needed them to leave out any chicken. While relaying that to the proprietor, I had a feeling he refused to believe what he just heard, because otherwise he would have some rather violent fantasies about me. To assure him that he had heard correctly, I called Dandelion inside to voice her own wishes, and she did it with a smile that melted the grumpy old man's heart in an instant. Inspired by beauty and innocence, he began to cook with a zeal and vigor that I had never seen in him before. I would like to make fun of his sudden change of heart, but I was just as enthralled by Dandelion as he was.

It is impossible for me to remember what I ate that evening, but I know I shared that meal with Dandelion, sitting on the Indian place's windowsill, laughing and fooling around while the setting sun threw crimson rays down the length of the street. I remember cars clattering over the cobblestones of the unpaved road, their metal reflecting some of the dying sun's light onto Dandelion's golden hair, giving her an otherworldly sheen, a literal glow that was only reinforced by her flush cheeks, her curious eyes and her beaming smiles.

Once nothing remained of our food, we went back to my flat. I half expected her to get her bicycle and drive home immediately, but she came inside with me without a second of hesitation and we got comfortable on my couch, her head resting on my shoulder as the light of the day faded.

We kept talking through that evening and this
time the content of the conversation stuck with
me.

She talked about her mother and grandmother
she lived with. About how they were very
traditional people and almost always
disapproved of things she did, while pressuring
her to be a perfect little princess. They were very
successful at doing this, I might add, for
Dandelion was precisely that. A spoiled, well-
behaved and somewhat shy but simultaneously
curious little princess. She was stunningly
beautiful, successful not only at competitive
dancing, but also at playing the violin and horse
riding and she was about to finish a very good
school education. All this was her nature,
nurtured so thoroughly that it was hard for her
to break away from these princess-patterns of
behavior. For example, it was utter bliss for her
to sit on my couch, lean on me and enjoy my
company - but at the same time, she could not
help having a bad conscience about having
feelings for an older guy and actually being
alone with him at his own home. Not the kind of
bad conscience where she was worried about
explaining this to her grandmother if she ever
found out, but the kind of bad conscience where
it made her entire being frown upon herself.

Luckily, she was in exactly the phase where
this type of girl begins to realize she has lived in
a gilded cage all her life and becomes curious to

leave it.

So she stayed, cuddling against me while telling me tales of her life.

One such tale was about her dance partner who had been scouted in another country by her trainers. He had come to visit once and he had... taken some coercive liberties with her. Her first real erotic experience, and even that had only been a one-sided service performed on him. Still, it had left a bitter mark on her, an uncomfortable memory she could not shake and a worry about this future dancing partnership that was unfolding between them.

She also told me, to my slight dismay, that she had met with one of my friends the day before, after visiting her grandparents. We shall call that friend Simplex, for he was always - and still is - a dull and simple fellow. Simplex and Dandelion had been breaking corona quarantine rules for quite some while now, first only to practice dancing routines while her actual dance partner was at his home, half a continent away, but over time also to meet more leisurely and spend some friendship time at a local lake together. With her being completely inexperienced in romantic matters and him being as dense as the interior of a woman's traveling suitcase, it had taken them months to realize they harbored feelings for one another. Until the past day, that is, when he had kissed her (on the day she'd originally been scheduled to meet me!) apparently rather spontaneously during their training. She had been too perplexed to really give him any reaction he could work with and he had probably been so nervous that her non-reaction proved deafening to him and concussed him out of commission, for they had simply continued their dancing routine after an awkward pause and acted as if nothing had happened for the rest of the evening.

She now confided all this in me, someone she perceived as an expert and master in the art of flirting, and asked for advice. Always eager to teach wisdom to those in need, I pushed my burgeoning jealousy aside and began by enlightening her about the easy conclusions I could already draw from her little story, like him being nervous and insecure, her not giving him any signals he could work with and some more elemental things. These observations were revelations to her, gods bless her heart. I believe without me, she would have brushed that kiss and all the other moments of affection off as just his way of friendship. In fact, not all her assumptions had been benevolent. She also asked if it was possible that Simplex is "one of those guys" who would only enjoy a girl for a short time, merely pretending to offer a serious romantic relationship before moving on to the next skirt to chase. I assume that this was a bogeyman placed into her mind by her doting mother and grandmother. I am rather convinced that I could have given oil to those fears and doubts of hers, nipping that relationship in the bud before any stronger emotions could blossom, but alas, I have never been a ruthless man and, as the reader knows by now, rarely manage to act in my own interests.

I was, however, exactly "one of those guys" who looked for physical gratification without offering a long term emotional bond. And I immediately told her that, to prevent any later misunderstandings from crashing down on us.

And this was the point where she showed at least some maturity of mind.

"I know. But you're different. Simplex acts like he is a friend and he kisses me to indicate he wants more than friendship, no? He would not kiss me if he was not serious about me. With you... With you I know from the beginning that you have someone else, someone you love. I know that this is just something for us to enjoy, this time together, this hand on my leg, this way you're looking at me. You're not making any promises you could break."

I knew there was more to come, so I silently kept that gaze on her that seemed so enjoyable to her.

"I just... never thought it would feel so good. And I never knew that you were allowed... that we could even do this at all. Otherwise I would not have waited so long!" She was close to tears at that point, and I pulled her towards me, her face against my chest, her arms around my body and she helplessly squeezed against me, torn between her feelings for me and this beginning love for Simplex, torn between the princess that finally found a prince and the adventurer who only just realized that she could explore herself, too. No tears were spilled there, but I waited for her to regain composure nonetheless, postponing the question that had formed in my mind: If she had never known that my relationship allowed for other girls, how had she found out now?

She answered before I could even ask, mumbling her immediate thoughts into my shoulder.

"Lily was right. It is impossible to let go of you, once held in your arms."

"I spoke to her, you know. We got to the topic of boys and she asked whether I know you. I said I've known you for a while and that I always somewhat fancied you and she was beaming with joy, telling me she's also in love with you and then told me about the things you've done and the things you were about to do and I... I just sat there, speechless and confused. When I finally asked her about Rose, she explained this thing you do, she called it an open relationship. And it just hurt so much to realize that this kind of thing exists and that you're doing it and that we could have... all this time we could have done this."

"You spoke to her? When?" You see, dear reader, when I have a beautiful girl in my arms, crying because she loves me too much, my immediate concern is not to console her, comfort her and wipe her tears away, no. It's to interrogate her about her friend in the psych ward that I was not allowed to love.

"I talk to her a lot. We're friends, you know. She doesn't have many others to talk to. And it's so sad that bad things always happen to her. I love her like a sister, you know." Funny, that. I was also forced to love her like a sister.

"So do I. And I'll always be there for her if she needs me. Same goes for you, by the way. I like you. I like you a lot." I kissed her forehead.

"You're not angry? About me seeing Simplex yesterday? About me falling in love with him?"

"No. I could never be angry with you." Oh how young, naive and wrong I was. "And I'm rooting for you to entrance him when you see him again tomorrow. If you manage to make him yours, I will always be here to give you advice. And if you fail, I will come over to console you immediately, okay?"

She sniffled, gave a nod and buried her face in my shoulder again. We sat there for a while, until she consulted her watch and suddenly jerked up, realizing how much time she'd spent here already, then mumbled something about her mother worrying.

So we got up, she got into her shoes and she stood on that little step where my front door is, now standing at eye level with me. We were still chatting about some inconsequentials, my hands on her sides and hers around my neck. Both of us dancers, we began a cyclical movement with our hips, swaying from left to right with a slight rotation, increasing and decreasing the touching area constantly, while still looking one another in the eyes and just talking to prolong the moment.

I slowly got closer to her, until both of us could feel the other's breath on our lips, waiting for her to make the final step and initiate contact.

If young men are reading this story, I would generally advise you to view me as a negative example and that you do not try to imitate me or use this as a guidebook to follow. The one thing you can take away and incorporate into your own behavior, however, is to offer kisses instead of taking them. That moment when they realize you are giving them the choice is as liberating and empowering for them as the moment of contact when she decides to meet your lips with hers is triumphant and celebratory for you, because you'll know they really want this and are willing to share, or even completely take the blame for it.

In Dandelion's case, she decided to let the moment pass untaken. Despite her airheadedness, I know she recognized the moment for what it was and also realized that the choice was hers. She also knew that she would enjoy this. Yet still, the moment passed because of her conscience and her decency and I cannot help but commend her for it.

"I'm sorry, but I really think this is as far as we go today. As close as Simplex and I have gotten, even without being in a relationship yet, I think this would overstep something."

I may occasionally paint Dandelion in a somewhat dim light, but I have friends who reached the ripe age of thirty and still never realized you could respect the feelings of a person without being in a relationship with them. She was certainly more mature in that moment than they've ever been in their lives.

Backed by the near omniscience granted to me by hindsight, I now know that I still could have picked her up right there, thrown her onto the bed and begun with kissing her neck and the evening would have turned into a sleepless and exhausting night, full of carnal discoveries for her and given me exactly the triumphant and soothing experience I needed to heal some of the bleeding wounds that my heart and soul had taken from the battle about Lily.

But, and I realize that I am repeating myself, I have always been one to respect a rejection.

So I kissed the backside of her hand and bade her godspeed and goodbye, for she had said she felt like a princess with me and I thought she deserved to enjoy that feeling for as long as I could possibly evoke it in her.

Shortly after that first date with Dandelion, I was surprisingly blessed with a visit from Lily. No longer confined to the psych ward, she had resumed her dance training and needed new dancing shoes. Rose had more shoes than she needed and, still maintaining a healthy friendship with Lily, wanted to give her a pair. Rose was already storing most of her belongings at my flat, which I found insufferable but she ignored me whenever I reprimanded her for it. It proved to be a blessing for me on that day, because it meant that Lily had to come to my place to pick up her gift.

I was only warned a few minutes prior to her arrival and thus had had no time to emotionally prepare myself properly before I heard her knock at my door.

I opened it wearing sweatpants and a comfortable shirt, looking like a homeless person who was only house-sitting the flat for the real owners. She was looking impeccable, wearing shorts and a striped t-shirt, her hair bound together behind her head.

And in the blink of an eye, she entered, fell into my arms and pressed her lips against mine. That kiss lasted for half a minute, until she suddenly jerked away and threw a nervous glance out the door.

"My dad drove me. I'm actually terrified he could see us."

"He can't, unless his eyes are are able to

penetrate these walls."

I took her in my arms again, getting another long kiss out of her while sliding my hands underneath her shirt. She pulled away the next time we took a breather.

"Seriously. I am dead if he sees us." Another glance out the door. She smiled and waved at someone down the street. "No, damn it. Please stay in the car. What is he doing? He's just walking up and down next to the car. Stop being so irritating!"

I pulled her back in, closed the door and resumed the physicalities. She embraced it, clearly suffering from withdrawal, but despite the greed her body showed, her mind was terrified and she pulled away again, gently taking her lips off mine and my hands off her body.

"Where are those shoes?"

I handed them over.

"Thank you. We should really meet more often, now that I'm out of the psych ward." Another quick kiss, then she opened the door again, waved to her dad one more time and ran towards him with a very girly hop to her step.

Dandelion, meanwhile, had taken my teachings to heart and stolen that kiss back from Simplex the very next day after her stay on my couch. She then wrote to me in detail how it all happened and how happy she was and how thankful she was for my advice. She had asked him about his intentions and they had agreed that they were now girlfriend and boyfriend and, while not really knowing what to do with that yet, she was very glad to be in a relationship with him now.

Her mother and grandmother also agreed that he was a very handsome boy and a match to be celebrated.

There was only one problem, which Dandelion kept close to her heart and told no one but me about: He failed to make her feel like a princess and to evoke that flutter in her stomach, the way I so effortlessly did whenever she saw me.

Allow me to lead you astray, once again, onto a somewhat philosophical tangent. Or, more precisely, a bit of a wayward social observation of mine that affects the collective psychology of modern girl-boy relations.

In the far past, people used to say "a shoulder to cry on becomes a dick to ride on."

I can hardly confirm the veracity of that claim, being born in a new era where it certainly does not apply any more, but I would like to think that the existence of such a saying gives us a glimpse into the circumstances of bygone times. I am not confused enough to posit that this was an ironclad rule, a law of nature in olden times, far from it. But proverbs like the quoted one can only exist because enough people have made the corresponding experience and, upon hearing it spelled out, not only agreed with but also repeated the idiom further. To quote a word from a famous but fictitious pirate, I am theorizing that there are certain *guidelines* that the collective psyche adheres to, formed and shaped by external circumstances that affect almost every person in the observed cultural circle.

The advent of technology, especially digital message services, has severely upset these external circumstances when it comes to boys and girls. Where, heretofore, a girl that had worries and wanted to talk to a guy about these worries had to meet up with him, be in his physical vicinity and would certainly be subject to flirtations from him in return - for if he was not interested in her, he would hardly be listening - this led to a significant overlap in men whose shoulders were cried on, followed subsequently by aforementioned riding experience, even if that had absolutely not been the girl's original intent.

Now whether the riding part was coerced, convinced, seduced or forced is irrelevant to this thought experiment, the simple statement is that, before the rise of zuckerbergian communication, it was much more common than it is today that a girl would meet with a guy with non-carnal intentions and still ended up in very carnal convulsions between sheets and pillows.

This phenomenon has been widely eliminated by the prevalence of smartphones in today's society. Girls were granted the ability to separate shoulders from riders and frankly, I do not know why they have not embraced it with as much joy and celebration as they did the conception of contraceptions back in the day.

Almost every young man these days will confirm that he has spent hours upon hours writing with a girl at night, assuaging her fears and doubts about herself, discussing her worries and problems and, all through this, trying to evoke in her but a quantum of the feelings for him that he felt for her. Hope kept him going for weeks, months, sometimes years, always there when she needed him, but never called upon to satisfy the needs he really wanted to be satisfying. The reason for that is as simple as it is painful. While he was very well suited to be the shoulder to cry on, other boys and men proved to be much better steeds to ride. Others became lovers or even boyfriends while the poor fellow watched this unfold again and again, always hoping that it might be his turn next.

In my day, as young men, we called this the friendzone and there was much wailing about it and railing against it whenever another hapless victim was trapped in that merciless limbo right past emotional love but not quite at physical interest.

Dandelion, being a child of these modern

times, had correctly applied this separation and found one man to be comfortable and at ease with and one other to desire, whose mere presence would keep her alert and on her toes, who would look at her with the eyes of a predator and make her act like some sort of unnatural prey that was only pretending to run away, while secretly coveting the touch of those claws and the bite of those teeth.

Her great error, to the continued misery of everyone involved in this triangle of stupidity, was to form a romantic relationship with the former and a friendship with the latter.

You may wonder at the state of my relationship with Rose. Last you heard, we were at odds with one another, as she had just ruined the thing I wanted most in the world and I kept annoying her by putting the finger into that still-bleeding wound of jealousy.

But rest assured, we lived together in harmony, to the point that it would be boring to talk about it. With pandemic lockdowns fully imposed by the governing body, Rose had made a decision to temporarily move into my place, to avoid being a carrier that constantly connects the infections from her parents' colleagues to whatever I may catch from my own coworkers. The alternative had, of course, been to have her live with her parents and for us to not meet at all during lockdowns and we had both wholeheartedly agreed to move her into my flat instead. Life together was harmonious. We hugged each other through the night, kissed each other goodbye in the morning, both came home some time in the evening and then we either ordered food with my money or she cooked something for us.

We dearly missed our dancing evenings and parties with our friends, but we had one another and we found more than comfort in each other's arms. Without exaggeration, I can say that she was the main reason why I stayed mentally healthy through the coming years and the pandemic. And despite my brain continuously reminding me that she took Lily from me, I still loved her.

At this point, I had originally planned to summarize the next two years over the course of a handful paragraphs. Alas, in the process of doing that, I kept running into memories of events that deserve to be recounted in full, for your enjoyment as well as therapeutic reasons. As I am sure most of you have correctly surmised by now, I am using this story to work through some emotional troubles, to put it mildly. A political comedian once put it this way: "Many people pay good money to see a someone who listens to them ramble about their problems. Here I am, getting paid by all of you while you listen to mine such ramblings, and I think I got a vastly better deal. Except I can't lie down comfortably on a couch during my show." If I remember correctly, he used that setup for two more jokes. First, he admitted that this way of therapy didn't actually help him with his problems, then he added that this, too, is just like real therapy, since therapists would lose their customers if they cured them.

This book is my version of that sketch, or at least the part that I quoted word for word. The rest of his opinions, I strongly to disagree with. For one, therapy definitely is helpful and insinuating the opposite is bad taste at best and harmful at worst when it dissuades someone from seeking it.

The other point of disagreement is more of a hopeful one, as I believe that the exercise of writing this "out of my head" might truly be helpful for my mental state.

Watching my work day at the time may have led one to the conclusion that I did not have a lot to do, for I spent a considerable amount of it either looking at interesting stuff on the internet on my PC, or sending messages back and forth with Dandelion via my phone.

Concerning the work, let us say I had a talent for doing a lot of stuff in little bursts of effort, to then enjoy a bit of leisure in the time I made up by being good at what I do.

With Dandelion, on the other hand, I took my time. I had learned my lesson about autopiloting on the romantic tracks of life now and vowed to never do that again. I started off by writing a poem for her. It described a dream I'd had about her, dancing among the stars and nebulae of the universe like some celestial, glowing entity. To an innocent eye, it read like a romantic little imagery of a beautiful fairy-like dance, but knowing her to be somewhat dense, I filled it up with innuendo in the latter half. She did, of course, not catch that and instead beamed happily at reading it, saying she feels even more like a princess now than she'd already had before.

Things with Simplex were going at a snail's pace and her retelling the hardships of her relationship to me was hilarious entertainment. To put it quickly, she was still the picture of inexperience and aloof disinterest in the sensual and physical parts of a relationship, like these spoiled girls usually are. Simultaneously, she was very curious and, well, physically deprived but with her being a virgin, her body only knew it was lacking something, but had never experienced it before and could not communicate to her brain that it was in fact this thing that her personality had little interest in, that she really needed.

To add on that, the way her foreign dance partner had treated her on his visit had left some negative traces on her mentality towards anything sexual. To defend the poor young fellow a bit here, he had not been coercive but rather very persuasive and stubborn. Still, he had persuaded her to do things outside of her comfort zone and she had understandably been uncomfortable about it ever since.

Simplex, on the other hand, was an absolute victim of his past relationships and his own niceness. A man in his middle twenties, he was eagerly looking forward to the hotter phases of this relationship but whenever he clumsily tried to get any closer to that, she got squeamish about it and turned his probing caresses into handholding, closed her legs whenever his fingers got anywhere near them and consoled him with kisses and hugs.

This was fertile soil for my conscience to classify this as "not really a relationship", making it very easy for me to justify my continued flirting, although I would have done that even without casus belli.

This may warrant another explanation of my mental gymnastics, so please bear with me for a moment. A relationship is an agreement between two people, and in our case with Simplex and Dandelion, I was not one of these two people and not part of the agreement. Whether or not those two chose to uphold that agreement is a matter between them and no one else's business. I can of course decide to respect Simplex' feelings and yes I would feel remorse at sleeping with a good friend's girlfriend but I generally think that when your girl sleeps with another guy, you have a problem with your girl and not with the other guy. This whole notion of some social contract between all humans, an unspoken rule that we will all respect another person's bond is very foreign to me. Put differently: If another person's girlfriend wants to have intercourse with me, that already means 50% of the people involved in the agreement do not honor it. So then, why should I, as an outsider, respect it more than they do?

In the beginning of our flirtatious phase, Dandelion had been very hesitant to send pictures of herself. She claimed to be shy, saying that she had no confidence in her body and that the pictures would turn out dumb and bad. I then took a picture of myself, sent it to her and began to point out a handful of things I did not like about it. As expected, she said that all these things do not matter, reassured me that it was a very nice picture and that she would treasure it. I then told her that this is exactly the way she should look at her own photos and she went quiet for a bit.

I then received a picture of her standing in front of a mirror, wearing black shorts and a black top, both covering a minimum of body because she'd been outside in the sun. The caption was "you're lucky I happened to walk past a mirror."

I said she looked very tasty, complimented her on the tan and told her I really like her shoulders in that one. Very pleased with taking her selfie-ginity, I pushed my luck and asked her out to meet me after work some time this week, to eat some asian food at a somewhat hidden little restaurant. She agreed and I walked around with a grin for the rest of the work day.

Few days later, I finished work a bit early and drove to her place to pick her up for the date. She lived in one of the better districts of the town, right at the outskirts where you could quickly take a walk in the forest but also take public transportation to be in the city within ten minutes. That street is rows upon rows of single-family houses, each with a big garden and I spent my waiting time by gazing at well-trimmed hedges, well-kept front yards, well-maintained fences and all these things we expected to be a natural part of grown-up life back when we were kids and have no clue how to attain now that we are adults.

When Dandelion rounded the corner, you would not have guessed that this was an innocent and inexperienced girl. Her golden hair was practically glowing. Her black jeans were skintight, promoting her incredible physique, but without looking uncomfortable. They were adorned with little chains and torn in three or four places to reveal some of the leg beneath and to give it some rugged character. Her top was black wool, with long sleeves but a cut-out at the shoulders, something that pushes all my buttons and reroutes most of my blood away from my brain. (A little personal note here, to the one friend who I am certainly not trying to impress by writing this book: THIS is how you correctly react to me complimenting your shoulders.)

Her lipstick was subtle, her makeup barely noticeable and the glitter around her eyes seemed so natural, it made me wonder if that had always been there. Our greeting was a stormy hug, and she complained about some comment her grandmother had made about the outfit, which led to me immediately saying that she looked stunning and that I wasn't sure whether I could sufficiently concentrate on the traffic, with her sitting next to me.

She giggled, said that she was really happy to see me and off we went, driving to get some of my favorite Vietnamese food.

We ordered it to-go and took a little walk to the outskirt of the industrial area where this establishment was sadly and unromantically located. Still, I knew a spot right where the companies ended and the crop fields began, with a big wooden bench, some flowering trees and a bit of greenery. She asked for some of my peanut-sauce chicken, then blushed because she is a vegetarian. She quickly told me to keep this little cheat a secret, before adding me that cheating somehow felt less bad when she was with me. I didn't know what to answer, partly because I was wondering whether she even realized what she just told me and partly because I was simply mesmerized by the way the evening sun's rays got tangled in her hair and bathed this whole memory in a golden sheen that I always see when recalling it. I opted to say that she could always trust me with her secrets and she smiled at me and said that she had felt that about me from the day we first met.

We finished eating, then went on a little walk between crop fields and a nearby quarry, walking to a little vantage point where we could watch the sunset in its full glory. A deer suddenly bolted out from some shrubbery and rushed past us and I made her laugh by calling her a Disney princess. I held her in my arms until the sun was past the ridge, and in the evening gloom I changed from friendly and loving embrace to a more greedy and demanding grip, whispering into her ears that I had a few ideas that would improve this day, if only she did not have a boyfriend. She leaned back into me, increasing the physical intensity of the moment and asked me what kind of things I had in mind. One hand went underneath her top, fingertips touching her skin and sending shivers down her spine.

"I'd start like this," I said, biting her ear and taking her neck into my other hand, running my thumb over all the little hairs that were already standing on end. "And then we would decide on a direction to keep going into."

My hand under her top slowly moved upwards, over her ribs and towards her chest.

"But maybe I'll reconsider and go the other way instead." My teeth dug into her shoulder as my hand went back down, once more torturing her ribs before moving across her belly and sliding in under her pants and underwear. I turned her head with my other hand and offered another kiss, but this was the moment she shook herself out of her daze.

"That's… a bit too intense, sorry. You're amazing, but I don't think I can handle this yet." She smiled at me, still staying in this close embrace, but clearly projecting that this was where the touchy and greedy phase was at an end. I shifted my weight, turned this into a harmless hug again and faced towards the fiery red clouds that still reflected some sunlight despite the deepening gloom.

"That's okay. Just know that I'm always here for you if you want more of that."

I remember driving her back that evening, asking her whether she wanted to go to my home or hers. Fighting within herself, the innocent girl wanted to go home, do some studying and go to sleep early. The curious side of her that didn't want to be a sheltered princess any more wanted to come with me and see what other secret parts of her I could unlock. She told me as much and, unable to make a decision herself, left the choice to me. Rather cocksure, if you will excuse the pun, I drove her home and said that I'd prefer not to inconvenience her and that we had all the time in the world to continue this.

Thus ended our second date.

A third one happened soon after that, when some flirting led to her complaining about her grandmother again. Dandelion had colored some of her hair, adding reddish streaks into her golden mane and both her maternal guardians had been aghast at the sight. I said I'd love to see her new look, she sent a photo and I said that a picture was not enough. She immediately replied that I could pick her up in an hour and I sure went and did just that. When I asked what she wanted to do today, she just said we could get something at a drugstore and then go to my place. She bought some red dye, I got us some sweets and half an hour later we were at my place, her wearing black gloves and applying some more color to her hair while I was looking for a movie to watch. We spent the rest of that evening cuddling in my bed while her newly colored strands were drying, wrapped into aluminium foil. In the end, the movie of our choice was Pirates of the Caribbean and she kept swooning about Jack Sparrow, pardon, Captain Jack Sparrow. When the credits rolled, I got on top of her, kissed her shoulder and neck, then moved my lips towards hers, looking into her eyes while waiting for her to commit to the kiss.

"You know that I have a boyfriend."

"And you know you got into this bed of your own volition. And you haven't shoved me away yet."

"Because I trust you?"

"Because you're enjoying this too much to stop it?"

"Is that a challenge?"

And with that, she gently pushed me off, a wistful smile on her face.

She got up and went to the bathroom, to finalize the coloring of her hair, then we ate some snacks in my kitchen and when I tried to get closer to her one more time, she said she'd rather go home now. In my car, I kept one hand on her lap, while steering with the other.

"I don't understand why she goes for the smith guy and not for Jack Sparrow. He's so much more interesting!"

"You don't? But you're doing the exact same thing with me and Simplex."

"What do you mean?"

"You've got the nice guy on one side, who'd probably go to the ends of the world to save you but has no idea how to deal with your presence. The guy that your mother and grandmother favor. Innocent, meek, always respectfully distant and frankly quite boring. On the other hand, you have a guy that takes you out, flirts with your limits, takes what he wants and constantly tickles a side of you that you didn't even know existed. The personification of adventure, but you are refusing the call."

She was silent for the rest of the ride and I saw no point in piling onto that.

A few days later, she came to my place again, saying she wanted to study history for an exam and couldn't concentrate at home. I didn't mind the feeble excuse to visit me, until I realized she'd actually brought her schoolbooks and spread them out on my bed to study. I joined her, her belly on my bed and mine on her back, looking over her shoulder to see what she was reading. Me being rather versed in history and knowing that same exam and material from my own school days, we quickly turned that date into an actual history lesson. We went through the entirety of her school year with me providing either context or explanations and I do believe I significantly raised her final score.

Once finished, I tried to turn this into a more physical experience and for once, she happily obliged and went for the kiss. We made out for a bit, before she disentangled herself from me to lie down next to me. Ever mindful of the boundaries imposed by my partners, I did not greedily keep up the pace and instead just watched her breathe next to me, my hands playing with her legs. She pretended to be tired for a bit, but at some point her conviction clearly changed because she shifted positions, got closer to me and invitingly opened a path between her legs for my hand, where she had usually always been mindful not to leave any openings.

I took my time caressing her thighs, constantly looking out for any negative reactions. When my fingers finally reached the end of their route, she suddenly turned away from me, abruptly ending my hand's journey, and started crying into a pillow while facing the wall next to my bed.

I gave her space but stayed close enough for her to find physical closeness and warmth should she seek it and waited for her to calm down again. She quickly did, turning back towards me and wrapping her arms around me.

"I'm sorry."

"No, no, no. You are not the one that needs to apologize here."

"Neither are you. You just reminded me… I keep thinking of my stupid dance partner and the stuff we did when he visited. I don't know why this…"

"Sshhh. It's okay. He hurt you. Not physically, and he didn't mean to. But he overstepped your boundaries and that left a scar on you that hasn't healed yet. It's okay. I love the way you trust me and I want to help you with this." She wept a bit into my shoulder, and I kissed her forehead to soothe her, holding her until it was dark and late and she wanted to go home.

And the only thought on my mind, as I drove her home, was that I could fix her.

As usual, I told Rose about everything going on with Dandelion, once more expecting her full support, considering she had always advocated for me to try and meet with Dandelion in the years prior. She listened patiently, served me a second portion of her amazing stew, then looked me in the eye and told me that we need to talk.

"There has to be some boundaries. And one boundary is another person's relationship. You can't just do this with a girl that's taken."

"What? No, sorry. Their relationship is between those two. An agreement between Dandelion and Simplex. I never agreed to anything."

"Please. Find some decency."

"Why should I have more respect for their relationship than she has?"

"Can you see it from my perspective? We've both known Simplex for years. I see him every week during practice and I can't look him in the eye because of you."

"Honey, I understand your point. But you cannot break this. Not again. You've already killed my last chance. Don't do it again."

She was silent after that.

A few days later, she asked me to meet her at a local park, as soon as her university lessons were over.

We walked through the city, fighting over this topic, both repeating our arguments again and again, her close to tears, me getting angrier by the minute.

At some point, she compared this situation to the Lily disaster and accused me of always choosing other girls over her, evidenced by me not sitting next to her, back when we were at the movies. I told her she was being irrational and, most importantly, forgetting that I had literally asked her where she wanted me to sit.

With the argument entirely derailed now, we understandably got nowhere on the Dandelion topic. Since no agreement was possible in this state, she finally resorted to giving me an ultimatum to stop this fight.

"It's her or me. I know you're disappointed, but I can't handle this. Decide by Monday. I need to sleep at my parents' place anyway for the weekend because of a family visit." We both cried then, and she hugged me before saying bye until Monday.

People have complained to me a lot, over the years, whenever their relationships went sour. And whenever I heard that one partner threatened a breakup over something to win a fight, I'd thought to myself that I would never accept getting blackmailed like this. I had always known in my heart that I would immediately break up with a girl that does this to me.

At last, it had happened to me. And my resolve was shattered. I really thought about breaking up with her because of this voiced threat, but found myself unable to imagine a future without her. Now I am a man of vast imagination, I write novels after all. When I say I could not imagine it, I do not mean that a life without her seemed dull and very unhappy before my mind's eye, no. I could not see such a life at all. She had been an integral part of my life for almost six years at this point and she had been my reason to get up in the mornings, my cause to smile and laugh, my comfort in the night and my joy and pleasure in the flesh.

So after a few hours of deliberation, I wrote to Dandelion that I was very sorry to say this, but the flirting from my side would have to find an end.

She was devastated.

She complained about lost chances, told me the way I make her feel is something every girl in the world dreams of.

She lamented, once again, that we started too late and only really met when she was no longer in a position to embrace it.

She wailed and complained about Simplex and how she really loved him but he never managed to evoke this adventurous spirit in her that I so easily awakened with few words or light touches.

She called it unfair that Rose can just hog me to herself like this, then immediately expressed her understanding and explained that she would be just as terrified, in her position.

She told me she was terrified of losing me, that she only chose Simplex over me because she was sure I'd be there forever and that he was a chance she had to take or miss.

When I told her that I have until Monday to make a decision, she was silent for a while, then asked for specifics.

After some back and forth, she gave me the hint that her mother usually goes to sleep around midnight.

She said she would really hate herself for missing another chance with me.

She further complained that Simplex really didn't have any skills in the physical arts of a relationships and that she had been playing with the thought of asking me for advice or… instruction.

Not one to refuse an invitation, I told her I'd be there in an hour.

I still remember being too excited, to the point that I left the flat without either key to my car, nor my flat, forcing me to knock at my roommate's window in the middle of the night, during a thundering downpour, so he could let me back inside.

Finally fully equipped, I made the ten-minutes journey to her home, waited for a few more minutes for her to come out and then she was there, on my passenger seat, rainwater dripping from her hair onto her once again bare shoulders, with a wicked grin on her face.

"I'm not such a good girl after all, am I now?"

This will be another chapter that is physically gratuitous and can be skipped without missing major story elements.

Back at my place, I threw Dandelion onto the bed, tucked her into my blanket and held her against my body.

"We should really get warm first."

She giggled, sighed and rubbed her face against my chest.

When cold and anxiety had clearly subsided and I felt her become comfortable, I turned her head so she would face me and looked into her eyes for a very long moment, until she eventually spoke up.

"I can't do this, you know. It's so exciting, so tempting and it feels so right. But I can't do it to him. And I'm not brave enough to do it at all. Are you mad at me?"

"No, I'm not. You went this far outside your comfort zone to share your warmth with me in a secret night under my blanket. I'm happy, no matter what happens or doesn't happen now. And besides, I'll never be mad at you. Not once in our lives."

That made her cry again, for a short while. A mix of sad tears and happy ones, a mix of disappointed tears and relieved ones, a mix of resignation and defiance.

After calming herself down, she took my hand and moved it onto her breasts, rubbing one of them with it in a circular motion. I looked into her face and her eyes were begging me to take the responsibility away from her, to engage whatever I wanted to engage, to ignore what she had said before and to conquer her body and heart despite her mind's resistance.

And I broke through her defense like Iroh broke through the walls of Ba Sing Se.

I got on top of her, kissed her neck, her shoulders and finally her lips, always looking for signs that I'm overdoing it.

She showed none, meeting my physical needs with a passion that had been suppressed far too long and finally exploded towards me, greedily running her hands across my back underneath my shirt, constantly going for another kiss whenever I tried to move even the slightest bit away and even rubbing her hips up against mine with the rhythm of an experienced dancer. I decided to play her game, to continuously give her the familiar act of kissing, which seemed to be somewhat of a comfort zone for her, as even Simplex could manage that much, but rolling my body off hers and sliding my hand along her thigh, ever closer to her vagina while still keeping up the hungry kiss. Unable to say no, with her mouth occupied and unwilling to refuse me instead with her body, she allowed me to reach my destination unopposed. My fingers immediately felt the heat of her passion burning through the fabric and added fuel to that fire by aggressively massaging her. She did not moan and kept our lips pressed against each other's and her eyes closed - for a while. They were immediately wide open when I finally found the sweet spot to pressure, sending shivers across her small body and making the little blonde hairs on her shoulders and neck stand on end.

She finally ended that kiss, pushing me onto my back and mounting me, then greedily searched for a position of maximum pressure against the bulge in my pants. She quickly found it and I was once more allowed to watch a girl ride me who was home to the stable and the dancefloor, fully in control of her movement and body and an absolute beauty to behold. I ceded control to her, enjoying the view whilst only caressing her breast through her black top and cycling my crotch against hers to the beat that she imposed onto us, increasing intensity on her downswings and finally getting some moaning out of her. I reveled in my triumph for a while, before sitting up to face her and resume our kissing, which made her struggle to find the same intensity between her legs in this new position. I gave a raspy laugh, then threw her back onto pillow and blanket, pulled up her top and began to work on her belly with lips, tongue and teeth.

Slowly and with an eye out for any signs of overstepping, my hand moved into her pants, massaging her entrance again, this time through half as much fabric and with much quicker accuracy at finding her clitoris. I felt the tremors of her body when I kissed her well-trained and fit belly, felt her arching her back underneath me when I was biting her near her ribs and I heard her exhale sharply when I dug my fangs into her neck. Pulling my hand back out, I looked her in the eyes while working on her button and zipper, moving on to pull her white jeans off her legs and taking the socks with the same smooth movement, then probing at her innocent little underwear. Before I fully undressed her privates, I looked up one more time, and she was biting her lip with a mix of anxiety and trust, fear and love on her face.

Left with only her top on, and nothing beneath, she was lying on her back in front of me, her golden nether hair smiling at me, her tan, fit legs spread to invite me and her lower lips glistening with a hungry wetness, as if drooling in anticipation of my meat, once more allowing herself a cheat day with me.

I myself was drooling within my underwear as well, my clothes much too tight to control the hunger I felt for her, but my desires were not the focus of this night and I kept myself fully dressed for a while longer.

My hands locked around her burning thighs and I kissed her belly button, then drew a line with my tongue, ever downward until I reached that sweet wet entry point. Her gasps and moans spurning me on, I began by softly circling up and down her outer lips, avoiding the inner ones at first, despite them already laying bare. At this point, I was blissfully aware of the fact that we were treading completely new territory for her. The coercive dance partner had made her service him instead of servicing her and Simplex was clearly incompetent to even get her out of her pants. It was my intention to give her all the new experiences, all these stages of pleasure in little steps, making her reach a new height of ecstasy with every shift in technique, every new target I caressed and every new part of myself I'd use to do it.

I progressed from outer labia to inner, still going in circular motions. Next, we explored into her entrance, softly penetrating her with the tip of the tongue, reaching parts that will never know sunlight. After sufficiently exploring that area, we slid out for a bit, moving upwards to her clitoris, applying soft pressure with minute back-and-forth movement. Overwhelmed with pleasure, she forgot how to breathe and I was somewhat worried when she stopped moaning.

I moved off her, kissed her forehead, her nose and her mouth, then placed a finger between her legs to resume where my tongue had just been pressuring, allowing me to witness jolts of shock and awe run across her face again and again whenever I decided to increase the intensity by a little bit. When her body finally convulsed in an incontrollable shower of trembling shivers, I had the grin of a lifetime on my face and, at last, allowed the two of us a moment of respite.

Laying in bed, next to her, I drank in the sight of her as she breathlessly stared at the ceiling, before turning towards me with a look of adoration and awe that I wholeheartedly want every man to see from a girl at least once in his life. We intertwined hands, my left and her right, and just played with each other's fingers for a while, interlocking and opening them again and again.

"So, do you want to unpack your present and pleasure me for a bit? Or should I keep spoiling you?"

"Keep spoiling me," she demanded with barely a whisper.

This time, my finger entered into her, sliding so easily that I quickly added a second one. Always listening to her physical reactions, I soon found an adequate speed to penetrate her with, dictating to her a rhythm of pleasure that her whole body soon danced to. When it seemed that she had gotten used to this new feeling, I stopped aimlessly entering into her with each thrust of my hand and instead sought to massage the inside of her abdomen, running my fingertips over the tiny ripples of her inner walls, knowing fully well that each little bump I felt must have been to her like I was throwing her off a mountain. When even that stopped drawing gasps from her, I added another instrument to the symphony and began to lick her clitoris again.

Now some things I described here may surprise a few of the men reading and - sadly - probably even some of the girls and women who got their hands on this book.

"Ripples on the inner wall?"

If you are a man who does not know these, you have neglected your duties of exploration and experimentation and, frankly, your disinterest for female physiology and the ways to make them happy disgusts me.

If you are a woman and have never been devotedly massaged there in your acts of love, I dearly suggest that you raise your standards and stop letting numbskull idiots into your pants.

My great hope is that you are learning nothing new here.

My second greatest hope is that you are at least learning something.

In that vein, there will probably be another teaching here for many readers, in the next act described.

Dandelion did of course get used even to the double stimulation of my fingers inside her and my tongue's pressure on her sweet spot.

But I had one more way to impress, one more addition to the cacophonic overload of her nervous system.

Many men have trouble finding the clitoris at all, for which I have very little sympathy. But even those who routinely find and pleasure it know not the secret that lies beyond: What you feel there with your fingertips, and so dutifully massage to get shivers and climaxes out of your partners is only the protective layer. Underneath is the true sweet spot, a place where women are so sensitive that every tiny touch feels like an earthquake to them. That little tip of pleasure is usually hidden away, not only underneath aforementioned protective layer of skin, but also by retracting into the body. Once aroused, this part extends and a small part of it becomes accessible from the outside.

This was my next target.

I pulled out my fingers again, which resulted in a sound of disappointment, then put both hands between her legs and guided the thumbs to the right place with my tongue. I carefully slid away that protective layer that I had massaged for quite a while now, then used the underside of my tongue to probe and feel until I found the desired hub of stimulation.

This is important. The underside is by far the smoother part of your tongue and in this one place that makes a world of difference.

When I finally found that tiny little spot, feeling to my touch like a polished but soft little pearl, I began a circular sweeping motion on top of it that sent Dandelion's body into a frenzy. I quickly realized that this was still too much for her and stopped my efforts, kissing her chest, her neck and then her mouth once again before taking her into a safe and warm embrace.

But an embrace was not what she wanted or needed. She pushed me onto my back, opened my pants and went to ride me again, my painfully bulging underwear pressed against and almost into her body. She kept that up for a while, mindless and animalistic until her strength ran out and she collapsed onto my chest, breathing heavily. I endured this for a while, her weight uncomfortable despite her size and my greed and hunger hard to resist.

It was time to stop resisting.

I moved her off me, got up to take off my shirt, my socks and my already opened pants. She was watching me, eager, terrified, hungry, excited. As I stood there in my underwear, I turned towards her again.

"The last bit is yours to unveil."

I once again needed another show of consent.

But that was not the game she played here. She needed me to break her defense. She needed me to take the blame off her, to take her and make her mine. Because she would not and could not give herself to me. This whole thing could never be allowed to be her fault.

And when I realized that, in that moment, I pushed my luck one more time, telling her to get on top of me, her legs around my head and my crotch in her face, so I could spoil her with my tongue once again, while simultaneously waiting for her curiosity to get the better of her. I knew she would take him out eventually, if he was right in front of her, like a packaged present that she only needed to open.

But she only blushed and called it a rather embarrassing position that she was not ready for yet.

Now make no mistake. This was still a situation where I could throw her on her back, take out my parts and penetrate her in missionary until the sun comes up. I've said it before, she wanted to be taken.

But I was exhausted. And I was very happy with the night so far. We had broken taboos, crossed borders, boundaries and limits by the score and she was clearly madly in love with me.

"I feel like should have your first time with your boyfriend, so we'll call it a day here."

And with that, I took her into another embrace, pulled up the blanket and I was the most satisfied man in the world.

She would celebrate her 18th birthday shortly after that night, and I my 28th.

To those who skipped again: This time, innocent maidens were indeed penetrated. She was certainly innocent, absolutely still a maiden and, yes, my fingers found their way into her body. Actual intercourse was not consummated, however, as I found a conscience in the last moments and told her to have her first time with her boyfriend.

I will suspend the usual linguistic niveau that I have carefully cultivated throughout the script up until this point, to be perfectly crass with you just this once:

I was a fucking idiot.

The gates of St. Peter stood wide open before me, an angel was literally smiling into my face and I refused to enter heaven unless carried through.

I have shied away from summarizing and shortening, in an earlier place, but the rest of Dandelion's story is a headache-inducing mess and she was never meant to be focus of this story in the first place, which makes it rather bewildering that she occupies more than a third of it, up until this chapter.

When I drove her home, she asked why Simplex never does the things I did that night. I waited silently, not immediately able or willing to answer and she went on to say that he never does the stuff I did with my hands or with my mouth today and she didn't understand why.

I told her that he couldn't. For one, he lacked experience and skill. I stressed that this was not a flaw and that she should embrace this as a chance to discover lots of things with him, together.

Then I told her she was scaring him.

"Today, you put up some defenses, instinctively, automatically. Some of that is natural and all girls do it. Most of it is because of the stuff your dance partner did. I was repelled by those defenses before, too. Today, I overcame them. But that's not an easy thing to do, for a good guy. And if there is one thing where Simplex is certainly the better man than me, it's being a good guy. He's terrified of doing something wrong and you are confusing him into stunned inaction."

"But how do I stop doing that? It just… happens."

"One way would be to come to my place more often, until you get used to the touches and the intimacy, until I make you forget you ever had bad memories associated with sex…"

"But you're not allowed to do that."

"I'm not."

"Then what's the other way?"

"Patience. You just have to give him - and yourself - many many chances, until you're ready to let him pass unopposed or until he realizes your opposition is so much weaker than your love. But that's something you two will have to figure out among yourselves."

They never did.

And if I could set the heavens aflame for that irony, you would be waking up to the red sheen of an inferno, to skies crackling and bleeding.

They were in that relationship for more than two years. She traveled a lot, seeking dance partners in different countries (yes, she was that good) and you could make the excuse that he could not always follow her. But he mostly could. And mostly did. They spent months living in a sunny southern country, sharing a flat and making a couples-account on a popular social media page, posting photos of themselves in funny poses, near landmarks, romantic old buildings or at a beach. They did a soft and comfortable winter photo shoot at home together, right before Christmas. They later moved to a tropical asian country, spending two months together in quarantine on a holiday island before being allowed into the country proper.

And yet, after she finally broke up with him, there was one evening she spent lazily lounging around on my bed. Where she found a condom under my pillow. And then she said this:

"A shame. Simplex and I never really got to the point where we would need one."

And neither did I. Her flame for me sputtered out, her attention span too short and her ability to fall in love only outdone by her talent for falling out of it again.

I became that shoulder to cry on, the guy who praised her for her triumphs, the man whose advice she could ask for, then ignore. She called me her "magical friend" and I was the guy she would text or ring up whenever she felt lonely in one more country of this world.

She lost that virginity soon after breaking up with Simplex. To some guy wearing makeup and tattoos who hit on her at the karaoke bar we frequented with friends. She later admitted that his looks reminded her of Jack Sparrow.

By his own account, he was too drunk to perform that night. She really couldn't tell the difference, beaming as she told me about that particular achievement. When that guy showed no further interest in her, which is his usual modus operandi as I later found out, she took another guy from that bar to bed for a few times before getting bored of him and moving on to one of his friends. I lost track after that, no longer interested, no longer asking her about her life. Right now, she's more than eight timezones away from here and, yes, she still occasionally asks me how I'm doing, what's weighing on my heart and what my dreams are, but I am at a point where I file her under "distant acquaintances". The girl I fell for does not exist any more.

None of that is meant to disparage her. I

respect her for making her own choices, choosing her own goals and making great strides in this world and her life. You correctly surmise that I do not usually agree with the options she takes, but none of that diminishes her quality as a person. Gods know, no one has an obligation to live their life to fit my imagination.

But it made me lose interest in her and this is the chapter where we close out her part of the story.

You may wonder what kind of story this is going to be. With some knowledge about dramaturgy, you might be thinking that a comedy should end in a wedding and a tragedy in a funeral. Now this story will have deaths and wedlock, yes, but not at the end of it and neither of them will be pivotal or climatic. If I was making all of this up, we would probably end it with a murder spree where I hunt down those who have hurt the people I love, before permanently exiting the stage. But that particular story has been done before. And since this is an excerpt from my life, there is no tension arc, no crafted curve of suspension leading up to a big curtains-closing bang. Life's author is a miserable one, although I am occasionally stunned by his ability to put irony or foreshadowing into the script.

Not tragedy then. Comedy is debatable. If you have laughed a lot up until this point, then I am honestly impressed by your ability to find humor where I sure lost mine long ago.

Rather, I would like to coin a new distinction in the drama category: A Misery.

A story that starts out very optimistic, then misses a chance and another chance for a happy ending, slowly sliding into a level of mediocrity that in itself is not tragic, but compared to what could have been cannot help but feel depressing. And from that point, we slowly slide lower, a barely perceptible downward slope, spiraling towards despair without ever reaching it and without ever having that big drop that normally serves as climax for such a story. At the end, the reader is likened to that frog in the boiling pot that never realized the pot is boiling because we turned the heat up in such small increments.

Whether such a story can be enthralling or even enjoyable is up to the individual. Personally, I always found "Grave of the Fireflies" rather boring, exactly because that did not strike me as a tragedy but as the perfect example of a Misery. The irony in my comparison, of course, is that the sister does in fact die at the end. But where death in any medium usually comes as a shock and as a turning point, that movie made it come as a natural conclusion. She didn't die at the end of that movie, she died throughout the movie. When it finally happened I only felt glad it was over. But regardless of that, there are hundreds and thousands out there critically acclaiming it as the pinnacle of emotional movies. This allows me some hope that my story might also find a devoted following.

When Rose asked me, the Monday after my nightly adventure with Dandelion, what my choice was, I naturally said that she would forever be the woman I was going to marry and no other girl would ever change that. It was the only answer I could give. The only truth I knew.

Once again, she had taken something I really wanted and dearly needed. And once again, I knew that she was worth it. This time, I had been smart enough not to develop too many feelings for the other girl, so the blow did not hit as hard.

And if this sounds an awful lot to you like the last time I had to go through some mental gymnastics to not develop a grinding grudge towards Rose, you would be correct. For the blow was a lot lighter and softer than last time, but it struck onto a cracked surface that only strained further under the impact.

As a personal little bit of revenge, I kept my little midnight adventure with Dandelion a secret from her. A tiny vindictive action to keep my anger in check, breaking our sacred rule of trust and honesty. It was only much later that I found out she'd spent the same night with Diego and explored her own feelings about whether or not we should keep our relationship polyamorous.

Harmony continued, despite all our efforts. Rose did a great job organizing my birthday party that year, luckily on a date right between two lockdowns. She gracefully invited Simplex and Dandelion and even Lily, but Lily could not come.

That year went by without many more eventful days, as the pandemic picked up speed over the winter and our social lives all stopped happening. New Year's Eve was uneventfully spent in our flat with the roommate. One notable thing happened as we toasted to our upstairs neighbors with our drinks during the fireworks and they toasted back with a joint, then invited us up to share in the green treasure.

The next year began with a geopolitical event that more than quadrupled my workload and within weeks sent me into burnout.

At some birthday party that probably broke quarantine rules, Rose and I finally managed to both leave with someone we picked up during the party. She took some sporty guy who lived half a country away and only visited for that party. I took the young blond hospital worker who looked much better clothed than after I undressed her, whose blowjob only drained my enthusiasm instead of raising it and who I sent packing right after the act because sex with average girls is such an immense disappointment compared to a naturalborn succubus like Rose - or those nights where my desires had been within reach with Lily and Dandelion. I felt like I had wasted my first actual sex outside the relationship and felt soiled and stupid about it.

Lily spent the covid years in and out of the hospital and psych wards, even going to school there, between therapy sessions and group activities with the other patients. She formed close bonds with a few girls who shared her situation and then immediately lost one of those close friends to a suicide. This added more trauma to her inferiority complex and her rape and I cannot help but question the practice of putting troubled girls together to form these kinds of friendships when there are probably statistics out there showing that every single time you do this, one of the girls kills herself within years or even months, traumatizing the rest of the group. The remaining girls decided to draw at least some strength from that loss and gave each other an oath, solemnly swearing that not one of them would follow into those footsteps and heave her load onto the others by leaving them behind.

And yes. This is foreshadowing. Not that I could take any credit for it, this is the doing of life's author, not mine.

I have very fond memories of that second covid year, despite the burnout, despite the lockdowns and despite all these cracks widening in my relationship with Rose.

Four particularly happy days happened in the middle of the year when restrictions were lifted and we had what I call the "Summer of four Weddings".

The first of these took place in May. Two very good friends from our dancing circle who Rose and I had known before they had even been a couple were taking their vows at a rural hotel. They said yes in a little white pavilion, next to a little pond and despite a sudden shower of rain, everyone's faces were sunshine and smiles. We were surrounded by the same group of friends from that fateful Christmas celebration at the beginning of the story and that day is among the happiest of my life.

The second one took place one month later at a nearby rural castle. Two very good friends from our dancing circle who Rose and I had known before they had even been a couple were taking their vows in a small church in our home city, next to a priestess and an altar and despite the religious sermon, everyone's faces were sunshine and smiles. We were surrounded by the same group of friends from that fateful Christmas celebration and that day is among the happiest of my life.

The third wedding took place another month

after that, at a country-club-style restaurant in our city. Two very good friends who I had known from when I'd only started dancing and helped become a couple back then, were finally taking their vows in a gigantic church that the groom's mother was frequenting. The religious parts of the event were once more mind-numbingly boring, but at the party afterwards everyone's faces were sunshine and smiles. We were surrounded by some friends from our dancing circle and that day is among the happiest of my life.

The fourth wedding was in a lakeside restaurant and I had to endure Rose's alcoholic family throughout it. When dancing finally became an option, I could not even do that, to escape the wretched table we were seated at, because Rose had broken her ankle between the second and the third wedding.

I did not specifically mention this earlier because it was hardly an impediment to the enjoyment of the third wedding. We were surrounded by scores of enjoyable people there and whether or not we could dance did not have significant bearing on how enjoyable the evening was. It dampened the mood a bit, yes, but the mood was so good that it only made a barely perceptible difference.

At the fourth wedding, it ruined the one thing that could have saved it. Please pardon my hyperbole. It was of course still a nice evening and her family could be very funny at times. But her injury hung over that evening like a dark cloud.

That broken leg deserves an explanation, and since we are done with the Summer of four Weddings, I will take the time here.

You will remember how I said that Rose is capable of breaking anything, not out of malice or stupidity but out of sheer refusal to give the warranted care when handling breakable things. She managed to apply that concept at a birthday party of an old classmate, in spectacular fashion, by standing around, doing nothing in particular, then shifting her weight in a clumsy way. There had not even been any alcohol yet, although the mishap did not stop her from drinking and enjoying the evening anyway. She later served as a source of hilarity as most guys present were medical students and they formed a line to examine her, only for each of them to say they that they had not covered that topic at university yet.

But yes. One second of her usual carelessness cost this absolutely stunning girl, this dancer on the floors and in the pillows, this utter bombshell and beacon of positivity *everything.*

And when I say everything, I am, sadly, not exaggerating. She never really recovered. Deprived of the dancing hobby and ways to work out, she gained weight and lost motivation. Visiting her parents' "trusted" doctors instead of getting proper treatment meant that the pain never fully vanished and apparently liquids had gathered somewhere in her foot and weakened an important set of bones that could not heal properly. I do not remember the details.

By the time New Year's Eve rolled around again, I had acquired a side girl from our dancing acquaintances of old and she stayed over for a sweet night of love with Rose and me, giving me a triumphant beginning into a year that would leave me suicidal by the end of it.

We had also seen Lily once or twice, during the year of four weddings. She came to watch a tournament at our dancing school together with her mother. I tempted fate a bit, massaging Lily's back and shoulders, seated behind her while her mother looked on. Not stupid enough to engage in any suspicious touches, we nevertheless gave her too much of a hint when we could not keep our mouths shut.

"Damn, that feels good. We should do that more often. Is there a way to schedule with you?"

"For you? Always. You have my number."

Seems innocent enough, but Rose later said that both Lily and I radiated a feeling of intimacy that could be felt through the whole ballroom.

In summer, we visited once when Lily had gotten herself a dog to help her through her depressions. Rose and I took a walk with her and tested something she had learned during dog training, about getting him used to people that were strangers to him. Her parents weren't home and when Rose left the room for a bit, Lily and I were instantly glued together again, much to the loud protest of her dog. I don't know what part of that day was taught in the training, but that animal never grew fond of me.

Lily said that we should meet like this more often, as Rose and I left to go home.

She came to another dance tournament, quite a while after the first one and before that day she messaged me.

"Hey, are you there on Saturday? I'll be there with my mom again and… we need to be more subtle. She's been really suspicious of you since that last time."

I agreed, sad to have one more thing separate me from her but simultaneously intrigued by this cat-and-mouse game that was developing between us. I quickly found out that she absolutely was not able to play mouse. I deliberately took a seat away from her but she immediately waved me over to sit with her. When I sat down on the floor in front of her chair, she moved her leg in a way that did not allow me to ignore it. I kept caressing it for hours and every time I stopped even for a minute, she gave me a light kick in protest.

She took me with her when going for a smoke, leaving us one on one at exactly the same stairs where we had shared our first kiss and once she was done with her cigarette, we were locked in another embrace. This happened twice, and both times she broke the spell by claiming she needed to visit the bathroom. We did not go a third time.

We also took a picture of ourselves and sent it to Dandelion, who was in southern Asia at the time. I love that picture and I hold onto it as a valued keepsake, a reminder of sweeter times.

She got herself a girlfriend that year, too.

Through a bit of coincidence, I also got to know one of her friends, back from her time at the stables, who was in a relationship with a friend of mine. Said friend introduced us when he invited me and some guys to an evening of shisha at her place and I will introduce her to you as "Sunflower". Sunflower, because she was from a rural village full of farmers and because she never failed to cheer me up and brighten my day. That year, both Lily and Sunflower were invited to my birthday. Lily could not come, but Sunflower was there and immediately asked how I knew Lily, because she had seen her in the chat group I'd created for the invitation. I told her that we were friends from dancing and she raised an eyebrow but kept further questions to herself and only explained that she knew her from the stables.

That sums up the year, I think. Four weddings. One broken ankle. Two dance tournaments. Lily's dog and her girlfriend. My first Sex outside the relationship and my first side-girl later on. Sunflower's introduction.

The first time I saw Lily in the new year was at a local festival. Think big tents with rows upon rows of tables and benches filled to the brim with drunkards and girls that look like they skipped school to be here. The music is awful, the air is worse, beer is spilled everywhere and the food costs so much you could have ridden a rollercoaster three times for the price of anything that contains meat.

Lily loves these almost as much as she love medieval fairs.

This particular festival was located very close my flat, so Rose and I went there one sunny day, pointedly avoiding the aforementioned tents, but still riding one of the carousels and sharing chocolate-covered fruits with one another. We took a picture for our socials and left for home.

Lily immediately blew up Rose's phone, mad at us because we didn't tell her we were going. She would have loved to accompany us.

So when we went there again, the very next day, I told Lily in advance. It had originally not even been our plan to go, but friends had reserved a table and needed company to fill it up or lose it. They had only realized this problem hours before the event started, so we did not have much time to do any planning around it. Nevertheless, we dutifully came, but instead of sitting through that entire experience, I excused myself after half an hour and received Lily outside. She brought a girl with her, hugged me tightly, then visited our table with me to hug Rose. She quickly siphoned off some beer and went on her way again, leaving me to the misery of the festival.

The next time I met her would be on a warm summer day, when a friend from another country finally visited me when he was traveling the continent. Rose was out of town, which allowed said friend to crash at my place and on that sunny Saturday, I showed him around town alongside another mutual friend. We quickly noticed a lot of young people running around in rainbow colored clothes, with rainbow flags and all sort of rainbow-themed accessories, giving us the quiet suspicion that there was a Christopher Street Day going on in the city. Upon reaching the central square, this was confirmed by an assortment of tents, a big dancefloor, some exquisite techno music and a large population of scantily clad young people. Knowing that Lily would be there, I excused myself from my friends for a few minutes and walked across the greenery, hugging one beautiful girl who had "hug me" written onto her chest and kissing a cute little redhead that was wearing "kiss me"-shaped glasses. When I saw Lily's friend group sitting next to a tree, I sauntered over, hoping for her to see me approach them. She did not.

Upon reaching her, I gave her a friendly little kick and said "Hey Lily."

She got up and jumped into a hug. I caught and held her, happy at her stormy reaction until I realized she needed me to carry her so she could reach my ears inconspicuously.

"Don't do anything stupid. My girlfriend is sitting right there." I love her voice when she is whispering with clandestine importance.

"You're saying I could, if she wasn't there?"

She didn't answer that and instead opted to ask what I was even doing there in the first place. I truthfully replied that I'd been looking for her, then explained that I was in the city with friends and coincidentally stumbled upon this procession. She waved to my friends as I pointed them out to her and they waved back. I said goodbye and we guys went on with our day.

This was just a few days after her seventeenth birthday.

I took my two friends to another shisha party at Sunflower's place that evening, where I overdid the smoking with such severity, I got myself a carbon monoxide poisoning that killed my entire week. Rose did nurse me through that ordeal, but I felt less love from her than I usually had. Her care was still affectionate, but there was a dutiful aspect to it that I had never sensed before.

A few weeks later, Lily visited the two of us. And at this point, we will have to slow down again.

I was working from home, but it was a slow day and most of my workload could be postponed anyway. I knew Rose and Lily were spending the day in the city. Lily had apparently asked if she could see me, and Rose allowed it, so they came back to my flat together. I immediately turned all my attention away from work and towards her. She sat down on my bed, I made to sit opposite to her on my couch. She winked at me and patted her hand onto the empty space next to her, so I exchanged a glance with Rose and swapped over, sitting close enough to feel the warmth of Lily's body.

We talked for a while, then decided to get some food and enjoy the sun outside. Rose said she still had something to do and sent the two of us ahead.

I did not dare to touch Lily, on our way to the food stall. Instead, we exchanged some innocent smalltalk and she said I'd have to help her order because it was her first time eating at that franchise.

Once done with our order and packed with three sandwiches, I remember this moment at the streetlight where she stood next to me, both of us waiting for the little red man to transition into a green one. And as I stood there, I felt an immense urge to hug and hold her.

So I pulled her sleeve, to get her attention. She turned to me with a sad smile, then turned back towards the streetlight.

Any other girl there I would have simply embraced without any careful tugging. But she was special. And I was terrified of losing whatever it was that remained between us.

We joined Rose in exactly the park where I had that first Date with Dandelion two years ago and we had a fun little picnic. After finishing our sandwiches, the girls conjured colored threads from some bag and began to string them together into colorful accessories, while I just sat there admiring them and caressing Lily's thigh with my foot.

I still remember her mumbling something, which made Lily yell at me when I did not immediately react.

"She said that tickles! Stop it!"

"No, that... that's not how I meant it. Keep going." And Lily blushed. But the moment was ruined already. Rose had shown that she was still jealous and overprotective and as our old wounds bled red into the green, their blue threads were interwoven with purples, yellows and blacks. We didn't talk much for the rest of the stay and I soon had to go back to work.

When I said my goodbyes, Lily wistfully remarked that we should do this more often.

One week after my 30th birthday and one week before the planned party, I went to visit Atlan for a traditional breakfast.

We sat on his balcony, the pot between us on a little table, drank soda and ate our meal with a joy and bliss that can only come from good food in even better company. Afterwards, we enjoyed the weather and talked about an assortment of different topics, including the widening cracks in my relationship. When his cat jumped over from the branches of a tree, he introduced the adorable little animal to me. He had named her Aemma, and she was a beauty true to her royal name.

When Atlan's younger brother came over to ask for some medieval clothes for the medieval fair, the two of us spontaneously decided to join the little brother and his friends. The brother got an outfit and went ahead, we took some more time on the balcony, then tidied up our table and the kitchen and drove after him.

It was a truly blessedly sunny day and if anyone ever makes a movie out of this story, I will get irrationally mad at them for not making this day sunny enough. We drove between lone trees, under lone clouds and past lone little farms, ever further southwestward until we finally reached the parking lot in the middle of a wide green field that was already filling up around noon.

I took a picture of the big gate tower at the

entrance and put it into my socials as bait, then we marched into a world of knights and taverns, of swords and golden necklaces, of old buildings and older culture yet. We watched jugglers, listened to merry tales, looked at a withered map of the castle and then walked the ruins of the outer battlements. I was locked into a pillory and I had to wait for a maiden to kiss me until the sergeant could let me out again. Instead of young maidens, Atlan asked middle-aged men to kiss me and one father with two little sons laughed at the challenge and gave me a raspy, bearded smooch to my smooth cheek. With my newfound freedom, we ate at a Viking-themed place where Sunflower was serving. We were seated next to a young mother with tattoos and two very young children, accompanied by the woman's own mother who seemed altogether tired of having to raise her grandchildren. Well-fed, we then walked a tour through the craft stalls, giving our attention to smiths, cobblers, bakers and all sorts of work that would feel a lot more rewarding than officework does.

As evening drew closer, we secured ourselves a good spot at the tournament grounds, which we shared with an old colleague I'd randomly met and the friend who accompanied her. Soon after that, we saw the young mother from that food place again, the children clearly done with turning their meal into energy and thus hyperactive. We offered to share our vantage point with them and formed some sort of spontaneous family right there, one kid sitting on my colleague's shoulders, the other on a railing in front of Atlan to have a better view. The mother and grandmother were thankfully taking a rest on a bench behind us.

In the meantime Lily had bitten at my bait, texting me to express her jealousy at me being at the medieval fair already. I, in turn, sent her all the pictures I'd   taken that day and then sent her some videos of the tournament show.

That show lasts for more than two hours and I was blown away at how much storytelling you can do within the constraints of a jousting arena. Lily replied that I'm spoiling too much, so I stopped chatting with her and actually focused on the story, which became the cherry on top of an already cake-like day.

Our way home through that starlit night led us back the same way, past lone little farms, underneath lone clouds obstructing the moon's light and between lone trees to the left and right of the road. I talked to Atlan some more about the troubles of my relationship and how much I really wanted to marry Rose one day, but could never do it as long as she broke everything you entrusted her with. I talked about her slow but painful physical transformation, about how she herself was devastated at seeing herself in the mirror lately, with all the weight she'd gained after breaking that damn ankle. My friend was very understanding, said that every long-term relationship has a point past the honeymoon phase, but expressed his full trust in our bond and our ability to overcome these little hurdles.

I dropped him off at his home, drove towards mine and went to sleep at Rose's side.

And then, in the morning sunlight of the new day, Rose and I broke up.

For the sake of this book, it would have been very beneficial to have a screaming breakup fight with flying kitchen tools and insults thrown back and forth.

We did nothing of the sort.

When I woke up that day, Rose was already up and tidying the room. I blinked into the rays of sunlight shining through my window and threw a loving glance at her, recalling everything I'd said and thought about the relationship, not only during the last day but also during the last weeks. She looked back at me with a look of pained love, like she was searching for something that used to be there, something she could no longer find.

"Hey. Morning. I was wondering. Do we... need to talk?"

She sighed and nodded.

"Come on, let's eat first, then take a walk."

This had been our habit for more than seven years. Take a walk when discussing important things. Meet a bad day on a full stomach.

So I got up, got dressed and sat down at the dinner table, with tears suddenly streaming down my face, endlessly and uncontrollably. Rose did not notice, at first, still tidying up some art utensils she'd used the evening prior. When she finally realized I was crying, she immediately dropped her earphones, rushed over and took my head into an embrace.

"Hey, hey... it's okay. Can you eat? Or do we

go on a walk first? I'm sorry, I should have known you'd realize."

My whole life, I have been unable to consume food when stressed. And despite the fact that I had been getting somewhat tired of many aspects of the relationship, to the point where I had considered to end it myself, it was still gut-wrenching to be so suddenly confronted with the immediately impending expiration of a love that had lasted a third of her life and a quarter of mine.

She knew that, of course. The fact that she apologized for putting a meal in front of me in that situation proves an understanding and a love that will be hard to rival if I ever engage in another partnership again.

We put the food away for later. I got my keys and into my outdoor shoes and then we went into the most beautiful summer day I have seen in years. Ironic. You would expect the end of a lucky and happy era in your life to be heralded by rain and thunder, but instead we had the sun bearing down on our town with a relentless benevolence, the air warm but not hot and the sky not only blue, but occasionally interrupted by clouds that almost seemed like someone had placed them with an artistic mind and decorative intentions.

We walked to a nearby spot with a low wall that allows you to look down at a bit of greenery and a little stream of water and we stood there, admiring the view together for a few more moments. Alas, our original cause would not be delayed for much longer, and it was me who eventually broke the silence.

"It's not working any more, is it? You're no longer attracted and I'm no longer in love."

She had tears in her eyes, while mine were already flowing freely.

"It's been seven years," she said. "Even more. Most couples never even make it this far. I guess this is as much time as we got."

I was sobbing, with no way to reply.

"Please stop crying. It's breaking my heart. And we're in public, doesn't it bother you?"

"Shut up. This is the saddest day of my life and I will honor that by flooding these streets in saltwater."

She laughed and it was a sound as bright and warm as the day itself.

I don't remember much of the rest of that walk. I know we reminisced about the best days we spent together, making sure to commit those to memory and not just the dried up days near the end where we had avoided each other's presence more than we'd sought it. I was crying a lot, and for a tiny, mean-spirited moment I was wondering why she wasn't. But I instantly realized that she had probably been crying about this for weeks in advance and was simply further ahead in dealing with the grief than I was.

We walked past a split tree trunk and I remember saying that we were also experiencing a rift, just like that one. And then we stood on top of that trunk, each to one side of that rift. I took her hands into mine, then said that there were still ways to bridge such a rift, even if the original wound could not be healed.

Rose beamed at me with tears in her eyes that still would not drop and she said that I am the most emotionally intelligent person she has ever encountered in her life.

I doubt the veracity of that claim, but it still means the world to me that she said it.

When we came back to my flat, she asked to stay there for a week or two, because her room at home was occupied by a visiting relative. I was happy to oblige, as I figured that it would make the separation easier to bear if we slowed it down. I know better now. Breaking away from a love is always roughly the same amount of total pain. You can only choose if you want all the pain at once, then find ways to cope with it, or whether you want to receive it in little increments that hurt you again and again, with no regard for the progress you have or haven't made in dealing with the last blow and the one before that.

For Rose, one such blow came when she realized that my mom and dad would both have their birthdays in a month and she would not be part of that. Hit with the sudden realization that my parents, who had always welcomed and cherished her, would no longer be part of her life and subsequently that my aunt and cousins and grandmother would be gone with no way for her to say goodbye to them, she finally could not hold back her own tears and it was my turn to embrace and console her.

For myself, I was hit very hard when I saw a cake tin in the dishwasher that she had used to make a lemon cake for my birthday. The thought that she had already known we were close to our end but still spent hours in the kitchen to show her appreciation and love made me break down on the kitchen tiles, sobbing. She was very worried to find me on my knees and crying. Her relieved laughter when I, between sobs, told her what had caused my distress is a memory that I will cherish until my death.

After a few days, she claimed she was getting back pains from sleeping in my bed and began sleeping on my couch. We both knew that for a lie, but I was always mindful to give distance whenever demanded, accepting this as one more step in our slow process of separation.

I still woke up with her snuggled against me every morning.

Another sign that she was unable to commit to the separation came one late evening, when she dug her nails into my neck, pulled me away from my computer and bit into my shoulder.

"Want to have breakup sex?"

I wanted. We did. It was some of the best we ever had together, and she breathlessly said she would miss it, once we were lying next to one another, trying to regain our energy.

"Don't you have Marc now?"

"I do. And I think I already love him. He's certainly going to be the better boyfriend. But he will never. Match. This."

I have talked at length about the skilled hip movement Dandelion and Lily had learned from riding and dancing. But when Rose mounted me one more time, she displayed a precision at riding cocks that was acquired and honed by riding cocks and doing it well. The other two girls, for all their magnificence, could not hold a candle to her.

This was the last time Rose ever slept with me.

Soon after, we moved her stuff out of my flat, she returned her key to my door and with these physical rituals, our separation was complete.

I spent the next weeks in a bit of a daze. I had emotional comfort from friends and my dear family and I found physical comfort in two girls who I had been sleeping with for most of the year already. We will call them Tumbleweed and Dumbleweed, because one of them still drifts into and out of my life to this day and the other one turned out to be a stupid cunt. Still, there was an undeniable hole in my life that those two could not fill and I desperately tried to find distraction from it in boardgames, karaoke evenings and even by chatting with Dandelion again.

For the games, I joined a local group that occasionally got together and allowed you to almost always find semi-strangers to conquer Westeros with, enter Valhalla alongside or dominate the universe against. On one particular Sunday, I got up early for a round of Twilight Imperium, scheduled a bit before noon with two guys who could explain the game and two others with were supposed to join us for a round of five.

The explainers were already there when I arrived, setting up the board. The other two never came.

Now this is a game that takes hours to play, which is why we wanted to begin so early in the day. After short deliberation, we decided to play a three-man-round even without the other players. I put my phone and my purse away, got out of my pullover and was physically and mentally ready to absorb an hour of rules explanation, followed by an afternoon of cosmic politics and spaceship battles.

The game was a lot of fun and on any other day, I would mark this as a very nice and enjoyable experience.

But on this day, when I collected my phone after we'd stashed all of the game's material, I had messages on several app services.

All of them from Lily.

"Hey, are you free today?"

"Hey, look at the other messenger, I sent you a message."

"Can you reply in the next hour? I need to know whether I'm getting that train."

I answered immediately, but she was already home. Upon asking what the matter was, she only said that it's not relevant any more.

Two days later, she wrote again. This was three weeks after my breakup with Rose.

"Can you keep a secret?"

"Yes, of course. I promise I won't be shocked, either."

"Well… would you have time for me? Just a few hours?"

"Such a long story to tell? I'm open this evening."

"Doesn't have to be today. Truth be told, it's a simple problem. I'm single again. And I am super underfucked and you are the only person I trust with my body." I could not believe I was allowed to be this lucky again. She was still interested. And she cut right to the case. The butterflies that had been dormant in my stomach now fluttered with the force of a dozen hurricanes.

"I'm honored. You could always visit me. I work until late afternoon. But I'd even take some time off during the day, if that's better for you."

"During work hours??"

"For you? Yes. Easily possible since I work from home."

"Rose can never know."

"No one will ever know." Yes, I see the irony in writing a book about it. "Do you want to fix a day in advance? Or is it better for you if you can come over spontaneously?"

"Spontaneously would be best."

Few days later, she wrote again.

"Sorry, this week won't work out. I cut myself too deep and it's really painful."

We then wrote back and forth for a week or two, me inquiring about her physical well-being and her curtly replying that it wasn't good. After she'd recovered a bit, I suggested for her to come next week.

"Next Wednesday?"

"Yes, I have time for you."

"And we'll be alone?"

"Yes. There's no one here. My roommate should be at work until evening."

"Good. But I'm not sure about the time yet because I'm at training in the afternoon. I'll keep you updated."

You cannot imagine my elation at knowing she was about to visit me and we were about to fulfill some dreams I'd harbored and suppressed for three years now.

An even nicer surprise came on Tuesday.

"Does today work, too? Rather short-notice, I know…"

"Yes, it's perfect. My day is free and I could take some time off and end work early."

"Cool. I'll chat you up later."

I spent that day beaming and grinning from ear to ear, until the other shoe dropped a few hours later.

"LOL, now I got my period today of all times. lmao."

This is not hyperbole and not artistic liberty. That was her wording.

"That is unfortunate timing. Reminds me of the last time you were in my bed, years ago."

"Yes, I know. Makes me laugh, even though it's so stupid."

That killed the Wednesday as well, naturally. So I waited again.

"Hey you could come over this weekend." So

much for waiting. My patience was paper-thin, my excitement wearing heavy and my fear of losing her again was a terror that loomed over my psyche like Vesuvius over Pompeii.

What followed was a lengthy voicemail where she explained that her ex-girlfriend had called and that she was on the way to visit her, to talk about things one more time. She explained that there were still very strong feelings between them and things were kinda in the air again.

"So are you not interested in visiting me at all any more? Because you'd rather focus on your ex?"

"I… I really don't know that, right now."

"Because that would make this the worst day of the year, for me."

"I'm sorry. I really don't know what's next either."

"No pressure. I'm here if you need me. I'm here if you want me. And whatever you choose to do, I'm cheering for you."

I tried again, some days later.

"Hey, are you going to the festival in town?"

"No, not this time around."

"Want to meet me anyway?"

"Can't, my days are all full."

"What about next week?"

"Start of school. That's gonna make things difficult…"

"What about today?"

"My mom's birthday. But I'm so bored, I'll probably go to my room soon."

I gave up, after that. She had clearly managed to lose interest in me over the course of these few weeks. It seemed to me that I was simply not allowed to be with her. Some cosmic force obviously did not want us to find even a moment of happiness together.

"I'm in my room now. Sooo if we can't see each other because I can't visit you… what would you do to me if I was at your place?"

"Well I'd start with a few light touches, to see how you react. Put my hands on your hips when you're on my doorstep. Put my lips on your neck before you even enter the room. And the moment you lean into it and show me that you're enjoying it, I'd give you a long and hungry kiss."

What followed was a bit more than an hour of fantasies, once more exchanged via the same messenger we'd already used for this same purpose years ago. She was familiar with the way I would shape these and was a lot more engaged with it this time, giving me impulses and suggestions, turning this into a significantly more interactive exercise than last time. She was enthralled again, once more telling me she had an orgasm from my texts. I told her I needed a shower cause I was bathed in sweat, she said she was exhausted and needed to sleep.

A few hours later, she wrote again.

"I'm still absolutely done from what you wrote this afternoon."

"I could continue. Or you could sneak out and I could pick you up to make some of those dreams come true…"

"Wouldn't work…" A short break followed. "But you really killed me this afternoon."

"Well I'm gonna need more than just one round once we finally do it."

"That's gonna kill me even harder. But I guess we can do that."

"Don't forget that you can stop me anytime." A moment of silence followed. "Say, did you have any other guys in the last three years?"

"No, nobody. And damn you, just writing with you like this got me horny again. Help…"

"Help how? I already offered to come over."

"No, no. I really can't. But you could continue the story."

We then went for another hour. One more hour of interactive storytelling, controlled and focused from my side, accelerated and needy from hers. We found back to that desire that we once had and almost lived, back to that primal urge that made us want each other more than anything in the world.

"U did it again. I cannot move."

"The moment you step into my room, I am going to put three years of horny, three years of desire, three years of wanting to fuck you into that magnificent body of yours. We are going to

have three years of sex in one night."
    "I am dead after that. Dead and happy."

This kind of chatting went on for a while. She told me she never had a quickie and asked how I would do her with little time. She asked whether I could degrade her and insult her during sex. She asked if I preferred her shaved or natural. She told me she hates giving blowjobs.

When I casually mentioned to her that I'd met a girl for sex earlier that day, she asked what I'd done with her and wanted to know all the details.

She asked whether I was interested in older women and talked to me about her interest in older men. I joked that she was in luck, with me being almost twice her age and she said that's not what she meant and named George Clooney as a more fitting example. We talked about favorite positions. She said she wants it rough and wants to be dominated. She asked whether I ever got a girl to squirt and when I said yes, she confided in me that she and her ex never got each other that far. We talked about toys and she said she was curious, but never used any. But still, we never found a day to meet and in the blink of an eye, her summer break ended.

Saying that her return to school was detrimental to her mental health would be a grave understatement. For the last two years, she had spent her days at the hospital, alternating between therapy and small schooling groups with other troubled girls, done by trained teachers and mentors who knew how to work around their traumas and triggers. Going from that sheltered and thoughtfully considerate environment to the toxic heap of hormones and social pressure of a normal school killed Lily's motivation, her libido and frankly her desire to live. She needed increased medication to get through her day, took sleeping pills every evening again and abused   painkillers and Tavor to drown out the voices in her head. Whenever I asked if she had time for me, she only said that she could not do anything with me in this state and blocked all attempts at finding a date and time to finally meet.

My hope was already fading when, on an apparently good day, she sent this text:

"Hey I'll come over some time next week."

She then did not find the time on any of the five eligible days, leaving me more and more desperate, more and more terrified of losing her altogether again. I began to ask her about her schedule every week and when I finally asked her if that was annoying, she only said "yes, quite."

There was one more time of sexting, where I talked about blindfolding her and she shared some fantasies she had about Keanu Reeves, but even our digital interaction diminished rapidly.

When I went to watch a dancing tournament at her new dancing school, just to finally see her again, she noticed me the moment I entered the ballroom and immediately frantically texted me to say that no one could know about us here. At first, she wanted to ignore me altogether, but we then agreed that she would walk past me and give me a hug as a greeting. I was satisfied with a brief embrace and the smile I got out of her alongside that. The bigger solace to take away from that day was that in her mind there was still something between us that nobody could ever find out about. Even if I barely felt like there was anything happening at all.

Soon after that, she dropped out of school again, completely overwhelmed, overtaxed and overstrained by the cesspool of adolescence she'd been abandoned in. Back at the daily hospital sessions, she had even less time and headspace for me, denying every attempt I made at finally scheduling a visit to my place. At some point, I changed strategy, not asking whether she had time for me "next week" and instead asking whether or not we would meet at all during December, and even to that she said no.

Still, I kept up communication. Constantly asked how she was feeling. Constantly tried to tickle more interaction out of her. On a better day, we talked about her sleeping habits and she mentioned that only her best friend could ever sleep with her in one bed. Not even Lily's own mother was an exception to that, causing panic attacks in her like anyone else would. I remember saying that this detail would make our relationship even more complex than it already was, quickly adding clarification that by "relationship" I didn't mean to become her boyfriend, since I was absolutely not ready to give my heart into someone's hands again. I also said that I assumed she didn't want a boyfriend either.

She confirmed that with a short "u right", as had become her habit. Short answers, minimum amount of words, only replying when the conversation demands it.

December went by in a flash. I had, in the meantime, lost both of my side girls, Dumbleweed because she was a bit too crazy to stay with her, Tumbleweed because she was not crazy enough to stay with me. One would expect me to grieve the loss, but I still had high hopes about meeting Lily again soon, and compared to that, the other two were meaningless anyway. I have a bit of a suspicion that both of them tried to see the power vacuum left by Rose's departure as some kind of opportunity to usurp her old position and they had been equally met with disappointment upon realizing that I had no such intentions towards them whatsoever.

The one that actually hurt a bit was Sunflower, who broke up with her boyfriend at the start of

December, slept with me shortly before Christmas, then told me she was glad to have someone like me. I asked what she means and she said I was perfect because she really did not need a new boyfriend right now. Hearing that, I allowed myself to have some hope for her and me to keep this physically intense level to our friendship going for a while. Life's author must have been chuckling to himself when he made her meet with her next boyfriend on exactly the day after she'd said that to me between the pillows. This would really suit my kind of humor if I wasn't the butt of the joke.

I kept writing to Lily throughout the month, chatting with her on Christmas and wishing her a happy new year, to which she only replied with an thumbs-up emoji.

It was January that truly broke me.

I was still trying to find a date for us to meet and remained a weekly annoyance in her chat when she finally discharged the emotional artillery shell.

"Hey, uhm… I have a boyfriend now."

I was blindsided without mercy. The bullet took me over the cliff of mental stability and plunged me into the dark depth of devastation, doubt and regret without leaving me any foothold, any opportunity to soften my fall nor a chance to find my way back out and recover.

I had thought I was the only one she could trust with her body.

I had thought she had no time or headspace to meet anyone and that was why I never saw her.

I had thought that she really did not want a relationship.

And at this point, after all the grief she caused me, I still feel a need to defend her. Yes, she had said all these things and they turned out to be inaccurate. But at the point in time where she said them, they had still been true. Sometimes life just happens. Life happens when you drive your motorbike too fast and have to involuntarily decelerate with the help of a tree by the roadside, costing you two fingers and forever giving you a fear of biking again. Life happens when an unexpected job opportunity arises and you actually make it through their

screening process with flying colors, improving
your life quality and your salary drastically. Life
happens when you slip while descending from a
ladder and ram a nail into your palm upon
impact. And life also happened when Lily went
to the same castle I'd visited in summer, to see
the medieval Christmas fair and she met that
bard again that she had formed a friendship
with, years ago, even before her first
relationship, back at the tender age of twelve.

"It just kind of developed…" was her own
comment about it. She'd spent every December
weekend between the stalls and huts around
that castle, listening to his performances and to
those of his friends, then spent the remaining
time in his heated tent, presumably underneath
his blankets. It was the kind of love that would
not and could not be stopped and despite all the
jealousy I might have felt and definitely still feel,
I assume that she was finally happy, if only for a
few hours per week, because of him.

I, on the other hand, was as far removed from
any place of happiness as I could be, and in my
devastation and emotional isolation I had no one
to seek comfort from other than humanity's
oldest friend. In the form of rum, gin and wine
he was there when I needed him and never
denied me his company, unlike everyone else
who truly meant something to me.

To add insult to injury, salt to the wound and
acid to my mental space, that bard was older

than me by such a margin, you could have added her age to mine and still, combined, we would be younger than him. The man is ugly as sin, wears ridiculous outfits, spouts the most inane nonsense on various social platforms and as a chainsmoker, I imagine he must give off a smell worse than a morgue after three days without electricity.

Fueled by lonely misery and driven by alcohol, I naturally did not stop chatting with Lily, writing more and more dumb things that should have clearly gotten across how jealous I was. One evening, I annoyed her to the point where she rudely reprimanded me for it. Taken aback, I quickly sent an apology where I literally told her I was drunk and heartbroken and could hardly be held accountable for the things I was saying.

"But why are you heartbroken?"

Apparently, my emotions towards her had never quite come across, in all the communication over the years. She must have known that I loved her, at some point, but just as I had always been worried she might lose interest in me, I assume she'd held the same fear about me - eventually convincing herself that no feelings could remain after so much time and that anything that could or would happen between us must be purely physical, acts of release and gratification, devoid of emotion and attachment.

I replied to her question with something I'd been meaning to tell her for quite some time now, but had kept to myself so I could say it in person.

"You look at yourself, wondering how anyone could possibly love that. I look at you, wondering if it's even possible not to love you."

Of course, I never got any reply to that.

At this point, there was only one intelligent way to go about the whole situation. I had to sit tight, stop being a nuisance and wait for whatever moment in time where she would contact me again. Her relationship was long-distance, she was a schoolgirl who could not afford to frequently visit him and she had to keep it secret from her parents anyway, who she still lived with. The man was near fifty and his career depended on keeping a good enough image to perform in front of crowds and as much as he probably enjoyed her presence and body whenever she visited, the rest of his life must have been hounded by a fear of being found out and thrown to the jaws of public scrutiny. It could only be a matter of time until this union inevitably had to break apart, leaving her lonely, hurt and in dire need of someone who could help her pick up the shards of her torn heart.

Alas, this story has repeatedly reinforced that I am completely unable to act in my own interests and this time would not be any different.

For a while she still confided in me, a trusted friend, about her relationship. I kept asking to meet her so I could talk about all the things that still confused me and all the feelings I never got any closure for, but she kept blocking every attempt, either by saying she had no time or by ignoring my messages. Still, there was an air of familiarity and friendship to our texts that was arguably even an improvement to her short and dismissive replies from December and November.

Naturally, I found a way to completely ruin all of that in one fell swoop.

You see, it had been my habit to send roses on valentine's day, for years now. Three roses for Rose, one rose for every other girl I'd been interested in at the time. So when February 14th rolled around once again, I kept up that habit and sent a bouquet of ten roses to Lily's home address.

Stupid, at first glance. She was in a relationship, as strenuous as that connection may have been, and was in no position to accept any romantic feelings from me, no matter how beautifully I expressed them.

Even dumber at second glance, for this is the action I outright detest myself for whenever I take another disgusted trip through this particular avenue in memory lane. I tell myself that this part of the gift had not been intentional and merely a negative possibility that I was willing to accept as collateral damage, but there is a logical train of thought that should be laid out in full for you to adequately grasp the vile and destructive mindset I had been on at the time.

By sending an expensive amount of flowers to be delivered to her place, the house where she lived with her parents, I sent a clear message: Someone out there with an adult's income has at least a romantic interest in your underage daughter and at worst an ongoing relationship with her, which she is keeping secret from you.

She reacted via text, that evening.
"Did you send the roses?"
"Yes."
"Uncool."
"I thought it would make you smile."
"No, it didn't."
A break followed, where I was coming to terms with what I'd done.
"Seriously, that was really uncool of you."
"Yes. I can see that I am doing everything wrong right now. I'm sorry. I apologize."
"I don't want an apology. That doesn't help or fix anything. You are obviously annoying me more and more with every day and an apology would only add to that."
Women always complain that men are unable to take a hint. That was a hint, and definitely one of the clearest ones that men have ever received. Naturally, I ignored it outright and instead decided that this was the moment to pour my heart out to her.

What am I, to you?
What do you think when you see me?

I just… want to talk with you again.

I want to understand what that is, between us. Whether anything at all still remains between us. I want to know whether I've really destroyed everything we had.

I've done nothing but dumb shit, these last few weeks. Every time I send you another message, I think to myself "you fucking idiot. Leave her alone already!" But I just cannot do that.

Please, just one time, tell me what's going on in your mind.

"Sorry, even I don't understand how I was ever interested in you" would really hurt me, but at least I'd have clarity.

"Hey, I'd prefer to keep the friendship alive, but… you're making that very hard right now. And more than friendship just cannot work right now." I could live with that. At least I think so.

"I don't know how to even describe the feelings I have for you. I still care about you. But you're too… intense. And I am at a point of my life where I cannot deal with that." I'd like to hear that one. There's a beauty to that, even if it's still very sad.

"Dude, I only hit you up because I wanted to use you and had no one else. If I'd known what a lovesick puppy you were going to be, I'd have saved both of us the trouble and never sent that message." I would not even be mad to hear this.

I think my conscience would suffer pretty hard from this one: "Fuck you. I fell in love with you, three years ago, and you completely abandoned me for your relationship. This time, I'm the one with a partner and you're the one suffering. Suck it."

But do you understand why I want to talk to you? I just want to know your mind.
The fact alone that you asked why I'm heartbroken…

I'm even reading your favorite book right now, just to find some connection to you and to try understanding you a tiny bit better.

I'm really sorry about the flowers.

It took her an hour to reply to that behemoth of a message and she refused to answer any of my questions.
"There's nothing between us. That stuff a few months ago was just fun. Nothing more.

Nothing less."

After finally realizing that Lily no longer wanted anything to do with me, I stopped contacting her. Which I should have done months ago. Still, unable to completely give up on her, I kept following her on various social platforms to keep up with her life.

A few weeks passed with no communication between us, then Lily's best friend went missing. One of the girls she knew from the psych ward. One of the group that was part of their little never-suicide-pact. The one person in the world that could sleep in a bed with Lily without causing a panic attack. Immediately fearing for her friend's life, Lily began asking for helpers on every communication channel available to her, while simultaneously asking for her friend to come back.

I offered to drive her around by car, so she could check specific spots but Lily never replied to that offer and I left it at that.

Days went by, the police joined the search and some forests were combed with search dogs and even a helicopter, but there was no trace of her friend. An old classmate of mine works with the police and I gleamed from him that a suicide note was left at the hospital where the friend had been staying prior to her disappearance and that her phone was confirmed to be dead. After a few days, the police decided that chances to find the girl alive were miniscule and discontinued their active help. Lily continued the search, of course, even when she had to do it with only her ex and her mother helping her.

There was one other social post worth noting, right in the middle of that search. Lily and her bard had apparently had some argument and she posted snippets from it on her status. Details were unclear then and my memory is hazy now, but what I can say with certainty is that he broke up with her during the search period and he did it via phone.

Now I can forgive a man for having a happy relationship with someone I love. I might begrudgingly forgive him and harbor disdain for him in the depths of my mind, but I have said it before that I strongly believe that women should be allowed to decide for themselves who they love and who they want to be with. Up until this point, the man had done no wrong and I did not wish death or harm upon him.

But if he really took the one person in this world that could have made me happy, used her for three months and then dropped her the moment he felt her baggage… if he really discarded her during the most stressful and horrible time of her life, where she sorely needed someone to lean on, someone to take comfort in, someone to alleviate her pain, just because she was too much trouble for him to handle, then I swear this to all gods, all demons and devils, all cosmic beings and local deities who might be listening to our mortal little lives: He will die a slow and agonizing death and I will savor the memory of his screams until my own time comes.

The missing girl was dead, of course. It took a bit more than a week for her body to be found and all media immediately went silent about it, as should be done when someone takes their own life - especially at such an age.

Lily took it better than I expected, but that is owed only to the fact that I expected her to follow her friend into death. I honestly do not know how she made it through that ordeal alive and it is testament to a fortitude and strength that I know I would not have, were I in her shoes.

I gave her some distance after all that. A weird and obsessed kind of distance where I looked at her social media accounts every two hours. She was soon released from her hospital again and moved out of her parents' home into an apartment for troubled teenagers in the middle of my city, provided by some youth support organization. She went to school again.

One time, I saw that she wanted to go to another fair in our city and asked for people to accompany her. I was smart enough not to reply to that post, but I did ask Sunflower, who usually went to these kinds of events, whether she was going there that evening. She went with her boyfriend and some friends and I joined them, spending the whole evening nervously looking around and occasionally checking Lily's socials to see if she posted any pictures that could help me locate her.

I finally saw her at the exit when my group left for home and I stood just close enough for her to see me and wave or smile at me if she so wanted, but far enough to not be seen as intruding. She either did not notice me or ignored me and I never brought it up again.

I know we sporadically had some friendly chats again for a little bit, but I believe she only ever tolerated me when she was drunk.

At the start of summer, a bigger festival had its annual weekend in our city and some bands that

I knew Lily loved were scheduled to perform. I also knew from her socials that she had attended last year's iteration with her late best friend and I assumed that she would like to be there again.

So I contacted her and told her I was at the homepage to buy my ticket and I'd gift her one for her 18th birthday. She made clear that she would only go there with a group of friends and I told her I never even meant for us to go together. I just wanted to do this for her.

She agreed and I ordered the tickets, happy to know that we would finally meet again, if only for me to hand over her present.

Shortly after I bought the tickets, she was diagnosed with a damaged nerve in her upper arm, presumably caused by her still regularly cutting herself and going much too deep on one such occasion. She was quickly hospitalized again, then moved to another hospital so that a specialized surgeon could treat her and when she finally had a fixed date for the operation, it fell exactly onto the weekend of the festival.

I still attended with some friends. I sent her pictures, took some videos of her favorite bands and sent those to her as well. She thanked me for it, but she was down to one-word-replies again.

Realizing that I still annoyed her, I once again stopped talking to her unprompted and resigned myself to only replying to her public posts on social media. When she started making those public posts unavailable to me, I naturally still ignored the hint given and asked her out on the day of her birthday, to go to a bar. She declined, saying she was still in the hospital.

I then took a stroll through town that evening, with a bottle of cinnamon tequila, waited for midnight right outside her usual hospital and then made a little video message for her, singing happy birthday and toasting to her.

She replied to this one the next morning.

"Bro. I'm not even in that hospital."

"All the better, since I would have never entered and you would have never come out to meet me anyway. It's the thought that counts, isn't it?"

"Honestly, I'm feeling somewhat harassed by you lately."

"Alright then. Goodbye."

There it was. Finally. Not a hint, but a fatally clear request to leave her alone and exit from her life.

Which I did. I could not help following the remaining social media where she had not blocked me yet, but I did not contact her again and I began working on myself to find some other meaning in life, some other reason to get up in the mornings.

Not that I ever found one.

My mental decline must have been apparent. Friends began to worry about me, and rightfully so. Noticing some troublesome tendencies myself, I vowed to henceforth only drink on good occasions and in good company and that's an oath I've kept since. I began making dumb mistakes at work, which can either be explained by saying that I was distracted or somewhat more pessimistically by saying that I had lost all will do things correctly any more. I made a mortal enemy out of a dumb and frankly neanderthalian colleague during that time because one of my mistakes had to be fixed by her. I would almost use this occasion to apologize to her, if I thought she was capable of reading a whole book.

I still tried very hard to keep my social life going, kept attending our weekly karaoke evenings and attended local events with friends. Not because I wanted to, since there was no motivation left to do anything at all, but because the rational part of my mind knew that things would somehow get better again and I'd sorely miss having a functioning social cycle when that time finally arrives.

On one such events, a big weekend-long festival in the middle of our town, organized and supported by the city government, I was walking through the throng of people alongside my roommate and I ran into Lily. Or rather, I passed by her. She did not notice me, but my roommate had to drag me further, as I was paralyzed just by seeing her. I suffered through that whole evening, always looking around to see if I could spot her again, but at the same time terrified of that moment where I would finally find her and then not know what to do. Blessedly, I did not see her again. When my roommate's tolerance for strangers and events was exceeded, we turned back towards our flat.

And by some heavenly intuition, I stopped at the central square, where a local radio host was playing music as a DJ, and took a picture of the area to post into my socials. And before I could even put my phone back into my pocket, it vibrated for one little moment.

"Are you at the central square? I'm right at the front. And I'm alone."

A text from Lily. I almost dropped my phone upon reading it and I somewhat rudely told my roommate to fuck right off and go home alone.

He was rightfully pissed to hear that, but my capability to be considerate of others was gravely impaired and I brusquely waved him off. He finally understood that a man sometimes needs to do things on his own and left, allowing me to plough through the dancing, drinking and singing masses, through loud bass and the smell of sweat until I finally reached the fence at the front of the crowd, breathlessly looking around to find my promised treasure, my beacon of happiness.

She stood forlorn and lonely, a cigarette in one hand and a drink in the other, absentmindedly moving her hips to the beat of the music and nodding along. Her glasses looked oversized, her shorts far too wide and her beige top had no sleeves, putting her scarred arms on full display. Her hair was chaotic and her posture awful, especially for a dancer.

Despite all that, she was stunningly beautiful to me and I just stood there, drinking the sight in and preparing myself for whatever reaction she would show once she noticed me.

That reaction was a wordless and long embrace, leaving me close to tears in the middle of the city's biggest party.

We spent the next hour dancing, drinking and generally having a good time. I tried to get closer to her, of course, but she used cigarette and drink rather effectively to subtly signal her unwillingness. But while she did keep me away from full body contact, she still allowed a hand or two on her hips and leaned into that touch. My head was swimming and the alcohol was only partly to blame.

I loudly sang "I don't believe that anybody feels the way I do… about you now" while looking into her eyes and she made an especially sad face at me in return. A bit later, she faced me and said "hey, do you remember that Christmas party back when we first met?"

We reminisced together when suddenly a boy her age came tumbling out of the mass of people, said hi to Lily and asked her how she was feeling.

"As shit as always." They were obviously acquainted. It was clearly awkward for him to see her with someone else at her side and he profusely apologized for interrupting. Much too polite, I told him he was welcome to join us.

Sadly, the party ended around midnight, leaving the three of us to stand around looking rather lost as the crowd slowly dispersed around us.

"Can I accompany you home?" It was an evening for hope, if ever there was one.

"No, thanks. I don't think that's necessary." Hope squashed.

I then offered to dispose of the cup she'd been drinking from, since I had to dispose of mine anyway. I hugged her goodbye and before leaving, I turned to the young guy and told him to get her home safely. At least I could do that much, to soothe my conscience and fulfill at least some of the obligation I felt to keep her protected.

And then that boy said something that I probably misremember. Or maybe I misheard him the first time already and the memory isn't the issue. There is a high chance that the way this plays out in my mind was absolutely not what actually transpired. But if you ask me how that evening ended, my brain is fully convinced that he said this:

"No, please. You can have her today. You were here first, after all."

And although I doubt the accuracy of that memory, it haunts me in the mornings when I wake up, viciously chases me through the day and it is still on my mind when I go to sleep at night, forever taunting me with the implication that Lily was now the town's mattress, readily available for whoever "was there first."

I convinced myself that she had given up on love, after losing it again and again, either to death or to the stupidity of men and concluded that she had at some point decided to simply give herself to anyone who would want nothing from her but her body.

Which meant that I was disqualified, not because I didn't love her enough or because she felt nothing for me, but because love had become a chore for her, something she wanted to avoid at all cost. Except when drunk and alone, surrounded by drunker people and feeling unsafe.

I went home on my own, that day and I do not know whether that other guy actually accompanied her home. With some renewed hope, I began sending some messages to her again, but once more, she only gave single word replies and soon stopped answering at all. This time, I stopped contacting her for good, once I realized she had stopped replying. My only hope now was that she would still like me if we randomly met in the city or that she would chat me up again like she had done on that festival.

On one occasion, during our weekly karaoke nights, I drunkenly went into the yard behind our pub and, by sheer coincidence, realized that she lived in the same building I frequented one day out of seven, which makes me appreciate and curse life's writer one more time for his queer sense of humor. I was closer to her than ever before, now that she was completely out of reach.

I only met her one more time in my life, at another dance tournament. I did not expect to see her there because our dancing school organized the event and her rapist was participating as a contender, so I was once more shocked into paralysis when I saw her sitting there with her mother. Thankfully, some good friends were in attendance as well and not only dissuaded me from running up to Lily, but also distracted me from her throughout the day, so I would not constantly stare into her direction like some deranged psychopath. I did send her a little chat message despite my friends' protest, but she ignored it.

"Hi?"

Just as she ignored me for the entire event.

I gave up, after that. On her. On us. On life itself and on the hope that I might ever find happiness again. I still have that knowledge in the back of my head that I will be happier again, some time in the future. I have the knowledge that life happens, as outlined and demonstrated a few chapters ago and it usually does so without warning and unexpectedly. But knowledge and hope are two very different things and knowledge is all that remains.

So that's where the story ends. No climax. No showdown. As promised, the genre is romance misery and all we did was to slowly descend into a point of depression, making mistake after mistake and then inevitably reaping what we sowed. In the end, absolutely no one is happy.

Dandelion is an influencer now, or at least an aspiring one. I have no insight into her finances, but I know she spent a month in Dubai last year on a "business trip" that solved her debt issues. If you do not grasp the implication here, that is all for the better, but I will say that it does not bode well for her.

Rose does not dance any more. At all. Last I heard, the foot never fully healed. She also gained a shocking amount of weight and I know from mutual friends that she is a wreck, psychologically. The last time I saw her, she outright ignored me but that was fine by me because I would not have been able to keep the pity out of my voice, had we talked to one another.

Lily does not talk to me either, that much was covered in-depth in the last few chapters. Happiness, as always, eludes her entirely and I still believe I had a chance to change that when I first got to know and love her. She blocked me on one more social app, weeks after that tournament where she ignored me and for no apparent reason, as I had not sent her any messages in months. Even more paradoxically, I am still allowed to follow her on a few other apps and on top of that, I can still see that she is looking at every single picture and story that I share on my accounts.

As for me…

When I lost that job near the end of last year, I was almost happy about it. I really no longer knew from where I was supposed to draw the motivation and willpower to get out of bed in the morning, much less to walk through the city, dredge myself through public transportation and then spend eight hours with people I don't particularly like, while doing tasks that could be automated. Admittedly, the pay was an enticing incentive, but I had not spent any of my disposable income anyway, simply because there was nothing worthwhile to spend it on. There was nothing to buy that could raise my mood for more than a few hours.

I am also traumatized in a peculiar area of life: I am unable to put my phone away without getting nervous and terrified. This was caused by two events, both described in the story. The first one was the four deleted messages from Lily, back when Rose had broken our affair apart, right before Lily hospitalized herself. And then, digging into the same wound, that cursed Sunday where I put the phone away to play Twilight Imperium. And while I am fully cognizant of the fact that Lily will not contact me

any more, I am nevertheless terrified of missing
a possible message again every single time I put
that little portable rectangle outside of sight even
for just a few minutes.

In matters of love, I am utterly crippled. I am
constantly seeking someone who will give me
physical and emotional comfort, while painfully
aware of the fact that I would only use anyone
who romantically engages with me as a
distraction from the loss of Lily. Contrary to
popular belief, I do have a conscience and will
simply not allow myself to let anyone fall in love
with me. This has already led to multiple
situations where friends from different circles
later asked me, bewildered, whether I'm just
stupid or intentionally sabotaging my chances.

I am frequently told to change my outlook on
life and love and that my readily apparent self-
hate makes it hard for newer acquaintances to
form an attachment or even just a positive
opinion of me. Part of me truly believes that I
have used up all the happiness I was supposed
to attain in one life. I assume that therapy is in
order, but I imagine that a harem of attractive
and intelligent girls, each of them roughly
twenty years old, would instantly cure all my
problems and I would rather sarcastically and
half-assedly endeavor to work towards making
that dream a reality than spend two hours per
week in a dusty office, describing my problems
to some crusty old fart who has not felt love nor

lust in the last decade.

The only named person in this story who has a claim to happiness right now would be Diego, and even though he only played the most minor of roles in this retelling, he still deserves a paragraph to close out his story, if only because I have teased it twice already.

In a clear mirror to my story, Diego has had a perfect relationship with a beautiful and smart girl from the dancing school. But he fell in love with another woman. The kind of love that shatters your mind and has you thinking of that other person day, night, morning and evening. And, just like me, he met with that other woman, despite knowing it would displease his current girlfriend. His story led to the same crossroads, the same decision, the same fork of fate that I had so miserably tried to reforge into a spoon: Does he keep his existing happy relationship or will he choose this adventurous headlong dive into a new love?

I will once more quote his life motto, and yes I am doing this to mock him: "You cannot have everything you want. But you can want everything you have."

Now you might pause here and scratch your head in slight confusion. "Did I miss a part of the text? Was there some internal dialogue, some mental debate where our protagonist chose Rose over Lily? The choice was taken from him, wasn't it?"

And you would be right. Partially right. There was no specific point in time where I was given a choice, that is correct. But the choice had always been there, throughout those precious and cherished weeks at the beginning.

And yet, I had never even considered the possibility of leaving Rose. Through all the resentment caused by that three-sided affair, through all her blockading and obstruction and despite the roaring furnace of love that I had felt for Lily, it had never once even occurred to me that I could leave Rose for Lily.

But Diego, in my shoes, did just that. He left his girlfriend for his new love.

And that shattered something inside me. To be so suddenly confronted with the fact that there had been another option all along.

The beginning to this paragraph is a spoiler to the worst part of it all: Diego and his new girlfriend are happy together. They have that kind of intoxicating and contagious happiness that lights up every room the moment they arrive. I am not a miser and I am not jealous. I am swept along every time I see them and the evenings we spend together are instantly among my most cherished memories. But that high is fleeting and whenever I think of them in the solitude of my home, I only know that his example proves one truth that I simply cannot accept.

His choice was the correct one.

There is one more event that deserves a mention and I think it will serve well as the closing act on the story.

More than half a year after my night with Sunflower, she was in town because her boyfriend was watching the sports game at the stadium with his friends and she had been their driver. That left her with a few hours to kill in the city and we used it to buy some clothes for me and go to a café. There, she told me one peculiar story, from the first year I'd known her, back when she and Lily were both fifteen years old.

Knowing that Lily and I were familiar with one another and knowing that Rose and I were in an open relationship, Sunflower had, in an adolescent attempt at humor, decided that she would ask Lily what her connection to me was. The next occasion happened to be exactly that festival where Lily had been mad at Rose and me for not telling her that we were going there, you might remember that part.

So when Lily and Sunflower met there with a group of mutual friends, Sunflower asked Lily about me. Lily, of course, lied and said that I was merely the boyfriend of a good friend of hers. Now sunflower's whole joke was to also lie - and claim that she herself had slept with me. Lily had been visibly shocked and hurt to hear it and, without a second of thought, had replied that it's not possible, could not be possible and that she cannot believe her.

Sunflower was rightfully taken aback by such a strong reaction, knowing what she knew about Rose and me.

"Why are you so surprised about it? Don't you know they have an open relationship?"

"Of course I know, but…"

Lily never finished that sentence and the two quickly found some other topic, as that one had clearly become uncomfortable.

I never found out what exactly Rose said to Lily to break us apart, back in that damnable night after that magnificent afternoon. But the intensity with which Lily renounced even the possibility that I could have slept with a girl her age lets me know that Rose's words had occupied her mind constantly, in the following years. It gives me an insight into the love she truly felt for me and subsequently her disappointment at losing me. Hearing that little anecdote in that café, after everything was already over and lost, broke my heart one more time, when I had thought it could not break any further. I was left sobbing in public, with a confused Sunflower consoling me.

So what was my purpose, in writing down this story, this little memoir, this wretched excerpt from my life?

Is there a message in here? A moral? Maybe a life lesson?

None were intended. My own reasons are simple and disappointing, much like the story itself was.

I wanted to impress a friend.

I wanted to try writing a different style of language.

I wanted to finally write a story that I could finish and thought that it would be easier to write one that life already completed for me.

I wanted to get all of this off my chest, to write it onto the page and out of my system. I think it helped, although I'm still haunted by memories every night.

That was the working title of this story, if anyone cares enough: "What haunts the depraved."

There might be life lessons in here. If there are, I assuredly haven't learned them yet.

"When faced with a choice between someone who loves you dearly and someone you want more than anything in the world, you've already lost the former and should go for the latter" is really not a message I would want to leave to posterity.

There might just be a moral to be learned, but what is the value of moral when my best and moral acts are the ones that I regret the most in my life?

When I told a girl that she would never replace Rose, no matter how hard she tried.

When I told Dandelion to have her first time with her boyfriend and drove her home with her hymen intact.

When I accepted Rose's sabotage and continued my longstanding, trusting and loving relationship with her, instead of uprooting everyone's lives to be with Lily.

Three moments where I undoubtedly did "the right thing."

Three moments that keep me awake at night, three missed opportunities to reach a level of happiness that seems unobtainable to me now.

I keep imagining what I'd do if I could revisit those moments. And the worst part is, I know would do the right thing again.

If there is any advice to be gleamed from my story, it would be this:

You rarely have "a chance" with a person. Instead, you have moments. And yes, someone might fall in love with you and give you many moments, more than you can count. But they are always finite. In a relationship, as well as outside of it. And each one you waste, each one you do not grasp, each one whose full potential you do not fulfill will be lost forever. So whatever you have, whatever you seek, whatever you believe to be yours for certain, use the moments you are given.

Thank you. For reading this. For bearing with me.

If you want to reach out to me, try jackson.farway@gmail.com